"Marry Me."

Megan realized that her jaw must have dropped, because she suddenly became aware of the fact that her mouth was dry. Her thoughts raced around in her head like a rioting crowd of protesters.

Travis Kane was suggesting she marry him?
Travis Kane?

"Marry you?" she finally repeated weakly.

"I know you think I'm crazy," he replied hurriedly, "but just hear me out. We'll treat it like a business arrangement. We'll set a time limit—say for one year. At the end of that time we'll review the situation, decide if we want to continue the partnership. If we don't, well—who knows what will have happened by then."

He flashed that killer smile of his and she could feel herself succumbing to his reasonable tone....

Dear Reader,

We all know that Valentine's Day is the most romantic holiday of the year. It's the day you show that special someone in your life—husband, fiancé...even your mom!—just how much you care by giving them special gifts of love.

And our special Valentine's gift to you is a book from a writer many of you have said is one of your favorites, Annette Broadrick. *Megan's Marriage* isn't just February's MAN OF THE MONTH, it's also the first book of Annette's brand-new DAUGHTERS OF TEXAS series. This passionate love story is just right for Valentine's Day.

February also marks the continuation of SONS AND LOVERS, a bold miniseries about three men who discover that love and family are the most important things in life. In *Reese: The Untamed* by Susan Connell, a dashing bachelor meets his match and begins to think that being married might be more pleasurable than he'd ever dreamed. The series continues in March with *Ridge: The Avenger* by Leanne Banks.

This month is completed with four more scintillating love stories: *Assignment: Marriage* by Jackie Merritt, *Daddy's Choice* by Doreen Owens Malek, *This Is My Child* by Lucy Gordon and *Husband Material* by Rita Rainville. Don't miss any of them!

So Happy Valentine's Day and Happy Reading!

Lucia Macro
Senior Editor

Please address questions and book requests to:
Silhouette Reader Service
U.S.: 3010 Walden Ave., P.O. Box 1325, Buffalo, NY 14269
Canadian: P.O. Box 609, Fort Erie, Ont. L2A 5X3

ANNETTE BROADRICK

Megan's Marriage

SILHOUETTE Desire®

Published by Silhouette Books

America's Publisher of Contemporary Romance

SILHOUETTE BOOKS

ISBN 0-373-05979-5

MEGAN'S MARRIAGE

Printed in U.S.A.

Books by Annette Broadrick

ANNETTE BROADRICK

believes in romance and the magic of life. Since 1984, when her first book was published, Annette has shared her view of life and love with readers all over the world. In addition to being nominated by *Romantic Times* as one of the Best New Authors of that year, she has also won the *Romantic Times* Reviewer's Choice Award for Best in its Series for *Heat of the Night, Mystery Lover* and *Irresistible;* the *Romantic Times* WISH award for her heroes in *Strange Enchantment, Marriage Texas Style!* and *Impromptu Bride;* and the *Romantic Times* Lifetime Achievement Awards for Series Romance and Series Romantic Fantasy.

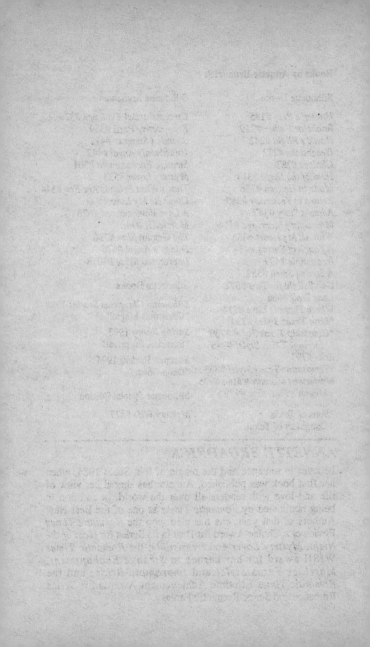

One

"**W**hat in the hell do you think you're doing?"

The sudden sound of a voice when she thought she was alone startled Megan O'Brien, causing her to sway. She grabbed the wooden frame of the windmill she was repairing to regain her balance before she looked down the fifty feet or so to the ground.

A late model pickup truck sat several hundred feet away. The relentless wind bringing spring to the central hills of Texas must have muffled the sound of the engine. Otherwise, Megan would have had some warning that she was no longer alone on that part of the family ranch.

However, no warning could have effectively prepared her for the sudden sight of the man standing directly below her, his Stetson shoved to the back of his head, his hands braced against his slim hips. Travis Kane was the last person she wanted to find glaring up at her while she clung precariously to the outdated relic that provided water—*when* it worked—to the cattle pastured on this section of the Circle B Ranch.

She stared at him with a sense of dread and frustrated dismay, wondering what Travis Kane was doing on the ranch. What could he possibly want with her?

"You got something against living to see your next birthday, woman?"

Anger at his high-handed, arrogant and demanding attitude shot through her. Who did he think he was, anyway, criticizing her, yelling at her? She rested her forehead against a crossbar, fighting to control the strong surge of emotion.

What more could happen for her to have to deal with? She sighed in disgust. For the past several weeks she'd been battling first one calamity, then another. She felt like a punch-drunk fighter, reeling from one disaster to another, unable to successfully cope with any of them.

The frozen gears of the windmill had been one more thing that had to be faced. When she'd discovered there was no water in the holding tank, she'd wondered just how many more things could happen. Well, now she knew. Travis Kane could show up.

Megan couldn't think of anyone she'd less rather see than the neighbor who'd spent most of their lives delighting in making *her* life miserable. Well, he didn't need to worry. Trying to run the ranch on her own had certainly added to her woes over the years, all without his help. She didn't need any more aggravations, thank you very much.

She glanced back at the rusted gears. The piece was shot—past being repaired. Somehow, she'd have to scrape up the money to buy a replacement part. The cattle had to have water out there, no question about it.

With a shrug at the silent question of where she might find some spare change for the part, she gave up her task for the moment. Concentrating on her footing, Megan began the long climb down the side of the wooden structure to the man whom she'd thought a scourge during her childhood.

"Couldn't you find an easier way to kill yourself than breaking your blasted neck?" he growled near her ear once she was within range. He wrapped his hands around her waist and swung her to the ground.

As soon as her booted feet touched the ground, she pulled away and turned to face him. From this position, she had to look up at the tall, dark-haired male who had spent their childhood causing her nothing but grief and frustration. She'd known him all her life—twenty-four years. Their families operated neighboring ranches.

The unexpected presence of Travis Kane was all she needed to complete a perfectly rotten day, that capped off a worse month and an abysmal year. She hadn't seen him in over two years. *Twenty* years would have been even better.

"What are you doing here? What do you want?" she asked, lifting her straw hat from her head and running her fingers through her short blond hair.

Although it was only April, the hot Texas sun was already causing her to perspire, despite the brisk breeze. She could feel a trickle of moisture slide down the valley between her small breasts.

Megan resettled her hat and watched him through narrowed eyes, waiting for some answers. She didn't have any time to waste on the man.

Despite his obvious irritation, Travis responded with a reluctant lopsided smile and shook his head. He tilted his hat forward so that it now sat low on his forehead, drawing her reluctant attention to his unforgettable eyes. They shone from beneath the shadowed brim with a resilient and mocking good humor, their deep purplish blue color reminiscent of the bluebonnets that covered Texas during a moist spring. Unfortunately Texas hadn't seen enough moisture in much too long.

"Well, howdy to you, too, sweetheart," he drawled, eyeing her grimy coveralls and worn shirt with the torn-out sleeves. "It plumb touches my heart to witness your excitement and enthusiasm at seein' me after all this time." He leaned against the windmill and propped a booted foot against one of the upright supports. "Can't you drum up a little neighborly affection for an ol' friend, honey?"

Megan peeled off her work gloves and shoved them into a back pocket of her coveralls. "You always were a pain in the posterior, Kane. I can't see where much has changed since the last time I saw you."

He gave her a level-eyed stare, his smile fading. "You know, I thought you had more sense than to clamber around like that out here by yourself. If you were to slip and fall nobody would know about it."

She turned away from him and started toward Daisy, who she'd left nibbling on a patch of sun-dried grass.

"You don't need to concern yourself about me." When she saw that he was following her, she added, "If I were you, I'd worry about my own neck. I hear you're still working the rodeo circuit. Not exactly a safe occupation to have."

"Those are calculated risks, Megan, whereas what you do is—" He waved his hand, as though at a loss to understand her.

She gathered up her horse's reins. "Look, Kane. I don't have the time or the energy to chat. I've got work to do."

"Damn it, Megan. I'm trying to talk some sense into your head. Will you listen?"

"I don't have time for you, Kane," she muttered.

He grasped her arm and turned her so that she was facing him. "You never do. As far back as I can remember you've brushed me off, treated me like I'm invisible. Well, fine, maybe I was a pest when we were kids. I'll give you that. I used to enjoy getting a reaction from you. You always were fun to tease.'' He waved his hand at the windmill. "But this is serious stuff, Megan. You have no business being out here by yourself, risking your neck that way. If nobody else will tell you, then I certainly will!"

His eyes glittered with suppressed feeling.

Megan glanced away from him before saying, "I'm deeply touched by your concern for my safety. Thank you for your no doubt well-meant advice on how I manage the ranch, Kane. I'll be sure to file it along with other words of wisdom that have come my way over the years."

She spun away from his grip and vaulted up in the saddle.

"Hold on for a minute, will ya?" he said, laying his hand across both of hers where they held the reins. "Don't be in such a hurry. I came lookin' for you because there's something I want to talk to you about."

Enough was enough! She didn't like to be manhandled and this was the third time he'd touched her since he'd shown up, uninvited, for this little social call.

She glared at his hand and fastidiously lifted it away from hers as though it were a snake. "Really? Well, I do appreciate the effort you've made to indulge in a neighborly visit, but I'm afraid I'm busy. Sorry, Travis. Maybe some other time," she added, thinking about the possibility of hell freezing over.

"What's wrong with the windmill?" he asked, ignoring everything she'd just said to him. He'd stuck his thumbs into the back pockets of his snug-fitting jeans, nodding over his shoulder.

She didn't have to follow his gaze. "It's worn-out, like everything else on the place. I'm going to have to order a new part."

"Why didn't you have Butch check it for you? Isn't that why you have a hired man, to do some of the more physical work around here?"

Megan wanted to scream at him, but she didn't. She held on to her temper, which wasn't easy, but she had learned long ago that losing her temper gave the other person the edge. She needed all the advantages possible around Travis. He had an unerring ability to get under her skin.

In a carefully even tone, she said, "It's not your business, but I'll tell you anyway. I was up there because the ranch is my responsibility. If there are any risks to be taken, I'll take them. Besides, Butch is too old to be climbing around up there."

Travis returned his gaze to her. "Better not let Butch hear you say that. He doesn't think there's anything he can't do."

Megan knew that he was right. Butch was one tough bird. "Maybe so, but I happen to know that his rheumatism has been acting up. He has no business taking chances."

"Neither do you."

So, they were back to that. She turned Daisy's head and started back down the track toward the barn. "Somebody has to do it."

"Damn it, Megan, will you wait up for a moment? I'm serious. I want to talk—"

She pulled on the reins. "You? Serious? Don't make me laugh. You've never been serious about anything a day in your life."

She gave her horse a nudge in her ribs and leaned forward, a signal that she was ready to move. Daisy, like the sweetly trained animal she was, responded beautifully, leaving Travis behind in a cloud of dust.

It was all Megan could do not to laugh out loud, especially after she heard his muttered remarks between the sounds of his coughing.

However, the urge to laugh was quickly gone. There was no reason to be taking her bad mood out on Travis, despite her dislike of him. It wasn't his fault that she felt like such a failure.

She couldn't shake the sense of impending doom that was with her from the time she opened her eyes each morning until she fell asleep exhausted each night.

Whether she liked it or not, she and her sisters were going to lose the ranch. It was only a matter of a few weeks now before the mortgage was due. Despite all her efforts, she would have to tell the bank manager that she couldn't make this year's payment. The O'Briens of Agua Verde County, Texas, were going to lose the Circle B after the ranch had been in the family for four generations.

Megan had been in charge of the place for the past eight years. She'd done everything she could to pull them through this bad patch, but it was more than a patch. For the past three years everything had been going from bad to worse.

She'd done everything she could, but it wasn't enough. It was never enough.

Butch was waiting for her when she arrived at the barn. "Did your company find ya?" he asked when she got off the horse. "I wasn't sure what to tell him other than you'd taken off to the hills somewhere. Where ya been?"

"Yeah, he found me. I was checking the southeast pasture and discovered there was no water in the holding tank. The windmill's frozen up. There's no way to fix it without ordering a new part for it."

"You want me to crawl up there and check it out, just in case something can be done?"

She shook her head. "I already did. The whole thing is worn-out. I need to replace the entire rig, but I can't. A new part will get us through the worst of the heat. Maybe by fall I can—" She stopped because there was no use talking about the fall. By then, the ranch would no longer be theirs... unless she could somehow produce a miracle.

A sense of futility swept over her.

They both turned at the sound of an engine and watched as a late-model pickup with Travis behind the wheel appeared. He made a sweeping turn and stopped in front of the house.

"Somebody mentioned to me yesterday that Travis was back in town for a few days," Butch said, rolling a handmade cigarette. "It kinda surprised me when he showed up, asking for you. I didn't think the two of you were exactly on good speaking terms."

She turned away from the house and led Daisy into the barn. Butch followed her, placing the newly formed cigarette behind his ear. "We're not," she said, leading Daisy into her stall, "but you know how Travis is. He just naturally thinks he's God's gift to us all and that we should feel honored that he decides to visit."

Butch uncinched the saddle and lifted it off the horse while Megan wiped her down. "So what did he want?"

She shrugged without looking around. "He said he wanted to talk to me about something. I can't imagine what."

"Maybe he got wind of the trouble you've been having. You reckon he might want to buy this place from you?"

She poured some grain into the feed trough of the stall. "He's not that stupid. Why would he want a place like this? He's never home. Besides, the Kanes already own a large portion of the county. Why would Travis take on another spread?"

"'Cause his pappy's young enough and healthy enough to be running their place for a long time, yet. Travis never was one to want to answer to anybody, not even his dad." Butch grinned at the thought. "Most especially his dad, if you want to know the truth." He stepped out of the stall and held the door open for her.

She motioned to the nearly empty feed storage bin as they retraced their steps to the barn door. "Did you remember to pick up the grain at the feed store today?" she asked, ignoring the fact that Travis now was leaning against the front fender of his pickup truck, watching, and making no effort to join them.

Butch took his time lighting his cigarette, then he removed his hat and carefully smoothed down his sparse and receding hair before replacing his battered hat. "Yeah, I got the feed. It's still in the back end of my truck. Ol' man Brogan said that unless you pay something on the account, he can't give you any more credit after this." He recited the message without inflection, studying the horizon.

"So what else is new?"

"It isn't just you, you've got to know that. Everybody in the county's been hit hard by this drought. It's been rough. They're all having to supplement the feed to keep the stock fed."

"I know."

"Ranching's never been a way to get rich, missy. It's a hard life."

"You aren't telling me anything I don't already know, Butch." Megan rubbed the back of her neck. "However, the ranch is my life. It's the only one I know. It's Mollie's and Maribeth's home."

He awkwardly patted her shoulder. "You've done a fine job, missy. A fine job. You took on way too much responsibility trying to look after the girls and run this place all by yourself, but you showed everybody you could do it. Don't feel bad if you have to give up now."

She stiffened at the mention of her sisters. "We've done just fine so far on our own. You just said it's nobody's fault the drought's lasted so long. Well, it isn't my fault that all our equipment seems to be breaking down at once, or that the blasted well for the house ran dry last month and we had to drill another one."

"I never said it was anybody's fault. Don't start gettin' so prickly. All I'm sayin' is that a young gal like you shouldn't have to be shoulderin' such a heavy burden. You should be out enjoying life with friends of your own."

She gave an unladylike snort. "My friends are mostly married and busy raising families. At least Mollie and Maribeth are old enough to look after themselves."

He nodded toward Travis. "So when are you goin' over to find out why he's hanging around here? He don't look like he's plannin' on going anywhere anytime soon, so ignorin' him isn't going to help ya none."

Once again she looked over to where Travis waited—his long legs crossed at the ankles, his arms folded across his chest—still leaning against his truck.

She glanced to the west before she spoke again. "I don't suppose this day could get any worse than it already has. I'll go see what it's going to take to get rid of him."

"I wish I had the money you needed. I'd sure give it to you if I did have it," Butch said in a gruff voice.

She patted his arm and smiled. "I know, Butch."

"I watched you girls grow up. I seen every one of you in diapers, following your folks around, playing with one another. Rory and June were always so proud of their girls. They wanted the very best for you. Always."

"I know. Sometimes life just works out different from what we plan...what we want." Straightening her shoulders, Megan turned away from Butch and headed toward the house, where Travis stood waiting.

Megan was aware of Travis watching her as she crossed between the barn and the house. She was well aware of what he saw—a skinny blond with a mop haircut, a plain face with a mouth too wide and, from the feel of it, a glowing, sunburned nose covered with a smattering of freckles.

Her coveralls were old, faded and wearing thin in some places, while her work boots were too scuffed to be able to tell their original color.

A regular fashion plate, that's what she was. She was also exhausted and totally out of sorts.

"So what are you hanging around for?" she demanded as she approached him. "What do you want?"

He slowly straightened in his lazy, loose-limbed way. "I told you. I want to talk to you."

She fought to control her impatience. She couldn't think of anything that this man could say to her that she would want to hear, unless he planned to announce that he was moving away from Agua Verde County and determined never to return.

Megan came to a stop a couple of feet in front of him and folded her arms across her chest. "What about?"

He glanced toward the house. "Couldn't we go inside and talk? This may take a while."

She didn't want to invite him inside. She didn't want Travis Kane anywhere around her, the house, or the ranch. Unfortunately, at the moment, she couldn't think of a single reason he would accept for asking him to leave.

There was no help for it. She'd just have to put up with him and the uncomfortable, itchy way she always felt whenever she had to be around him.

Megan stepped around him and led the way up the steps to the wide porch that led into the kitchen. "C'mon in. Mollie's probably got some tea made."

She walked into the large room that was the heart of the house. The kitchen doubled for the family conference room, the homework room, the problem-solving room, or for whatever reason the three O'Brien sisters needed to gain help and support from each other.

The place looked worn and frayed, now that she was looking at it through the eyes of a visitor. Any spare cash she managed to accumulate went back into the running of the ranch, unless it provided necessities for a sixteen-and eighteen-year-old to finish their high school educations.

She found the pitcher of tea, filled two glasses full of ice, poured the tea, then set the glasses on the round table situated in the middle of the room.

Megan waited until Travis sat down before she picked a chair across the table from him and carefully lowered herself. Lordy, Lordy, but she was tired. Not only was she not sleeping well at night, but she was also pushing herself harder with each passing day as though through sheer force of will she could turn the ranch's fortunes around.

Her body ached with every movement. She longed for a long soak in the tub and promised herself that particular reward for tonight in exchange for having to deal with Travis now.

Travis Kane had always caused problems in her life since she was a kid riding on the school bus. Why should anything be different now?

"So when did you get into town?" she asked, not really caring, but determined to curb her impatience and make a stab at being polite.

"Wednesday night."

"Mmm," she responded as noncommittally as possible. She picked up her glass and took a long, refreshing swallow of iced tea.

Travis waited until she looked at him before he leaned forward, his weight on his forearms resting on the table, and said, "I happened to run into Maribeth at the post office this morning."

She eyed him for a moment, waiting for him to continue. When he didn't, she prompted him with, "Did you?"

"She said y'all are having some problems."

She made a mental note to have a long discussion with her youngest sister about not discussing private family matters with outsiders. Striving for nonchalance, Megan shrugged and studied the ice cubes floating in the amber liquid. "No more than anyone else around these parts. Looks like the drought's about to do the whole county in.''

Megan made herself look at Travis, only then noticing that he'd removed his hat. Up close, his unusual eyes were even more noticeable, if possible, what with the stark contrast between their bright color and his tanned face.

"Megan—" he began, then paused, as though searching for words.

Megan knew that Travis had always had a way with words, so his hesitation surprised her. "What?" she finally asked.

"Maribeth says that since the new management took over at the bank, you don't think they're going to be willing to work with you on the mortgage payments anymore."

She could feel her jaw tighten at more evidence of her sister's loose-lipped ways. She took another drink of her tea before responding. "Maribeth has a big mouth," she finally muttered through clenched teeth.

He placed his glass between his palms and rotated it around and around in a circle. "Megan, I know you have no use for me. I'm not certain why, exactly. I mean, I know I used to give you a bad time when we were kids, but that was all part of growing up. I never meant anything bad by my teasing. I always thought of us as friends, even if we haven't seen much of each other in the past few years. I always thought that, if you ever needed anything, you'd know that I'd help you out in any way I could."

She shot out of her chair, knocking it over on the floor. "Is that why you're here? You think we're some kind of neighborhood charity case? Is that it? Well, you couldn't be—"

"Whoa, whoa, whoa!" he said, coming to his feet, his hands held out in front of him. "Damn, woman, do you have to go off like that over every little thing? What's the matter with you, anyway? Why would you take offense at an honest offer of help?''

She could feel her face flaming, which didn't help her temper in the slightest. "We don't need your help. We're doing just fine," she muttered, picking up her chair and replacing it on its legs. She sank into the chair and grabbed her glass with both hands.

"C'mon, Megan, it's me you're talking to. Needing help isn't anything to be ashamed of. We all need help at one time or the other.''

She looked up at him and knew she was making a complete fool of herself. Why didn't that surprise her? She had never learned to act naturally around this man, not even when they were kids. "I'm sorry," she muttered. "I'm just tired, that's all. I didn't mean to take it out on you.''

He sat down once again. "I know this is a tough time for you. I think you've done a hell of a job holding this family together. I just want you to know that I'm here to help you, if you'll let me. I've got money just sitting in the bank, drawing interest. I figure you could use it to help get over this bump in the road. Let's face it, we're bound to get some rain sometime. Cattle prices will be coming up. I figure you could be using the money since I don't need it right away.''

Megan couldn't sit there any longer, facing him. She got up from the table and walked over to the counter, her back to him. Never had her temper made her so ashamed. It didn't matter what Travis had done in the past, or how uncomfortable she felt around him. He had driven all the way out here to offer her a helping hand. And what had she done? Ignored him, left him standing in her dust, been rude and unsociable for no good reason.

It wasn't his fault that his good looks had seemed to make his life so much easier, that his irresistible grin had made all the girls carry on about him in school, or that she had received a great deal of teasing because they lived near each other.

It wasn't his fault that she didn't like him.

She picked up the iced tea pitcher and brought it back to the table, filling both their glasses. "I'm sorry for being so rude," she said, sitting down again. "It's really very kind of you to offer to help." Megan couldn't make herself look into those eyes. Hadn't they haunted enough of her dreams over the years without her being confronted with them now?

Travis leaned back in his chair and smiled at her in silent acknowledgment. "Dad tells me this new bank management team seems to be more concerned about their asset and liability reports than they are about the welfare of the people in the county. So you may be right about them," he said.

"Can you blame them? With some of the banks in the state going under, it's no wonder they're concerned."

"Have you spoken to them at all?"

She nodded.

"Did you offer to make interest only payments?"

"They aren't willing to do anything but accept full payment of all money due or to foreclose. Those are my options."

He muttered something under his breath that she couldn't understand, which was probably just as well.

Megan straightened in her chair. "Why do you care?" she finally voiced the nagging question that had been gnawing at her throughout the conversation. "Travis, you know as well as I do that we aren't friends. We've never been friends. It seems to me you probably expected me to fail. You never had a very good opinion of me, either, as I recall."

He rubbed his jaw. "I guess you're right. As far back as I can remember you've treated me like some piece of trash that was cluttering up your immediate area. I should be gloating about now that the high-and-mighty princess is taking a nosedive."

"Exactly."

They looked at each other for a long time without speaking. After several minutes of silence, Travis sighed. "I guess I deserved your haughty treatment, though, didn't I? I used to treat you pretty badly—pulling your hair, grabbing your books, making fun of your friends...."

"You made it clear what you thought of me, that's for sure."

"Would it help to remind you that I've grown up a little since then?"

He gave her that heart-melting smile of his that had gotten him out of all kinds of trouble as a kid.

"No," she said baldly.

"Oh." He looked around the kitchen before meeting her steady gaze. "The thing is, I was really shaken when Maribeth told me what was happening with y'all. I'd lost touch with you since high school. I mean, all that stuff I did to you was years ago. I've been on the road for the past eight years."

She knew that. He'd been two years ahead of her in school. She'd been sixteen the year he graduated. He'd been president of the student body, captain of the football team, homecoming king. By the time he'd graduated, he'd been driving to school for two years. So they were talking about behavior of more than ten years ago... almost half a lifetime.

"Will you let me help you, Megan? Please? Then I'll know you've forgiven me for all that childish stuff I used to pull. I can't stand by and watch you lose this place, not when I could help you. Surely you can understand that."

She couldn't believe she was having this conversation. Especially with Travis Kane, of all people. Of course she wasn't going to accept his offer, but the very fact that he'd made it blew her away.

Her silence seemed to spur him on. "You've done a hell of a job, Megan...keeping everything going. You were just a kid when you took over here. The girls were still in grade school back then, weren't they?"

"Yes." She looked away, absently drawing designs in the moisture collecting on her glass.

"When is the mortgage due?"

She glanced back at him, grateful that he had changed the subject. "The first."

"It's paid annually?"

"Yeah."

"It's no time to try to sell stock."

"Not at the current prices. Who knows if they're ever coming up. Nobody seems to be eating beef these days, according to present market indicators. I've been hanging on, hoping the drop is only temporary. If I sold at today's prices I'd lose everything I've invested in this herd."

"So will you let me loan you the money?"

"I appreciate the offer, Travis. I mean that. It was kind of you to hang around today when I was being so—rude. But, in the long run, borrowing the money from you isn't going to help. I would just owe another debt I couldn't pay." She rubbed her forehead where a headache was forming. "I've thought and thought about it. There's just no way out of it, no reason to prolong any of this." She forced herself to smile. "You know, it's kinda funny when you think about it. Paddy O'Brien won this place in a card game more than a hundred years ago, closer to a hundred thirty-five." She wondered if he knew that. "My illustrious ancestor was a riverboat gambler at the time. Didn't know a thing about ranching."

He didn't seem particularly surprised, but then few families in the county had histories that weren't known by all their neighbors.

"You've always been a gambler, too, Megan," Travis said in a tone more gentle than she'd ever heard from him. "Don't forget that. You're a fighter. A survivor. You never give up."

An unexpected lump formed in her throat. "Is that how you see me?"

"Of course. Why are you so surprised?"

"I always thought—" She decided not to tell him what she'd thought his opinion of her was. "Never mind. It doesn't matter."

He hitched his chair closer to the table and leaned toward her. "Look, if you don't want to owe me money, then I have a suggestion on how you could buy yourself some time—so that you could pay this year's mortgage payment, wait on the market to sell your cattle, maybe investigate other stock you might choose to bring in. It would give you some breathing room."

She eyed him warily. "What do you suggest I do, win the lottery?"

"Nope. Marry me."

Two

Megan realized that her jaw must have dropped because she suddenly became aware of the fact that her mouth was dry. She groped for the glass in front of her, draining it while her thoughts raced around in her head like a rioting crowd of protesters.

Travis Kane was suggesting that she marry him? *Travis Kane?* How could he be sitting there watching her so calmly?

"Marry you?" she finally repeated weakly.

"I know you think I'm crazy," he replied hurriedly, as though afraid she was going to demand that he leave, "but listen to me for a minute. Just hear me out. It won't be considered a loan that way. I'll be making an investment that may or may not work out, but whatever happens, you'll have the money you need, plus some left over. You'll have enough to repair that blasted windmill and whatever else's broken down. You'll have the money to hire extra help, which I'm sure you could use. We'll treat it like a business arrangement, like a partnership contract, or something. We'll set a time limit—say one year. Twelve months. At the end of that time we'll review the situation, decide if we want to continue the partnership. If we don't, well—who knows what will have happened by then?'' He flashed that smile of his and she could feel herself succumbing. ''I mean, the drought can't last forever. Things are bound to pick up and you won't have to be worried all the time about—''

''What's in all of this for you?''

He'd been talking rapidly but he stopped at her question as though a hand had been clamped over his mouth. He swallowed, eyeing her cautiously. ''For me?'' he repeated, as though puzzled by the question.

''Uh-huh. Why are you willing to be so generous? If you want the ranch, why don't you just make me an offer on the place and we can talk about it?''

''Megan, there's no way you'd ever sell this place and we both know it. This is your home. I don't want it. Ranching doesn't fit in with my life-style. You know that. Besides, if you sold the place, where would you and the girls live?''

She couldn't believe she was sitting there at the kitchen table having this conversation, and with Travis Kane, of all people. ''If we were to sell the ranch, we would have the money to move anywhere. If the bank forecloses, I'm not sure where we'll go,'' she admitted. ''But we'd find a place somewhere. We certainly wouldn't starve.''

''This way you could stay here and still have the money you need to make repairs and—''

''You didn't answer my question. Why would you make such an offer? What do you expect to get out of this?''

The look he gave her was definitely wary. ''A wife?'' he offered a little hesitantly.

"C'mon, Travis. The last thing you could possibly want is to get married. You need a wife like you need another hole in your head. And even if you've suddenly decided that marriage appeals to you, you certainly don't want to be married to me, of all people!"

He fidgeted. There was no other word for it. He pulled his earlobe, scratched his nose, fussed with his collar, then shoved his hair off his forehead. Finally he muttered, "Don't underestimate yourself, Megan."

Seeing his nervousness gave her some comfort, but not much. "Are you saying you're in love with me?"

He straightened in his chair. "Umm—well, would you believe me if I told you I was?"

"Absolutely not," she immediately responded.

He flexed his shoulders in another restless movement. "Then I'm not in love with you."

She gave him an approving nod. "Well, at least you're being honest."

He cleared his throat and took a long drink from his glass without meeting her gaze.

She studied him for several minutes in silence. "You can't be serious," she finally said.

"I am," he argued. "Try me."

"Try you?" she repeated suspiciously. "Would you care to explain what you mean by that remark?"

"It's just a figure of speech and you know it. I'm willing to prove to you that I'm serious, that I'm making an offer in good faith. I want to help you. That's what friends are for—to help each other."

"You make it sound like some kind of a game!" She leaned back in her chair and deliberately deepened her voice. "Hey, there's not much going on in my life these days. Maybe I should get married!" In her normal voice she added, "Life is always a joke to you. Admit it!"

"Well, what about you? You always look at life so blasted seriously all the time. Can't you lighten up a little, once in a while, have some fun?"

"Of course you would see things that way. Life's always been easy for you. You've never had to be responsible about anything or for anyone. You've never been serious about anything in your entire life."

"A few things," he murmured.

"Such as?"

"I've taken my rodeoing serious. I've won some good prize money. I take that serious enough. It's the money I'm willing to offer to you, money that I've worked hard to earn. You don't hear me joking about that, do you?"

Grudgingly she said, "Okay, I'll go along with that one."

"I take my friendships seriously, as well. I know I haven't been home much these past few years but whenever I'm in town, I've always made a point of checking on you, to make sure you and the girls were okay. As I recall, a couple of years ago I actually asked you to go to the movies with me. As also I recall, you were quick enough about turning me down."

"Going to a movie would have meant an hour's drive to the next town."

"Is that why you turned me down?"

She stared at him. "I get up early. I can't stay out late at night. I didn't figure you meant it, anyway. You were just trying to get a reaction out of me, like always. You've always been the biggest tease I've ever known, Travis, bar none."

"You don't date at all, do you?"

She looked down at her shirt and coveralls, then at him. "Of course I do. Why, I've got men lined up outside the door, impatiently waiting their turn to take me out. A stunning creature like me has to fight 'em off."

Travis frowned. "Don't, Megan."

"Don't what?"

"Don't make fun of yourself that way. You're a very attractive woman. Just as important, you're a very warm and loving woman, protective of your family, willing to do whatever it takes to keep everyone safe."

She narrowed her eyes and peered at him. "Did you by any chance get kicked in the head by one of those bulls you ride or something, Travis? I can't believe what I'm hearing coming out of your mouth. Are you sure you don't have me confused with someone else?"

"What I think is that we haven't spent much time together in the past several years and that there's a lot you don't know about me. Obviously what you do know doesn't impress you much. So how about giving me a chance to prove to you that I can make a good husband?"

A shiver ran over her at the word *husband*. Travis Kane? She would have to be out of her mind to consider marrying *him*, of all people. For any reason.

Even if it means saving the ranch? a little voice whispered inside her head.

For the first time in her life she finally understood what the preacher was talking about when he chose the subject of temptation for his Sunday sermons.

Temptation was a mighty insidious thing. It teased and tantalized, making all her beliefs dance and jump around, stand on tiptoe and fall over.

Travis Kane had been a pest as a kid, and his constant need to tease her had come close to breaking her heart in high school. Of course he'd never known the crush she'd developed on him back then. She had no intention of ever letting him know.

What would the star-struck girl back then have done if she'd known that someday in the future the ever-popular

Travis Kane would actually come to her and propose marriage.

As a friend.

He didn't love her, of course. Hadn't he just said so?

But then, she didn't love him, either. She knew better.

So. It would be a business deal, that's all. It would have an expiration date.

"A year, you said?"

"It can be longer, if you want."

"Oh, no. A year would be fine. It would give me some breathing space, like you said. I'd have some time to make plans, decide whether I should try to sell the place. After that, I could—" She paused, her thoughts finally leading her to ask, "I, uh—I guess you'd expect to live here, then?" She laughed nervously and answered her own question. "Well, of course you would. We'd be married and it would look strange to everybody if you continued to live at home with your folks." She knew she sounded rattled because she was. This was the most bizarre thing that had ever happened to her. Even more bizarre was the fact that she was actually considering accepting his outlandish offer... because the alternative was too painful for her to face. She'd been praying for a miracle, hadn't she? She just hadn't realized before God's strange sense of humor.

"I'm not home all that much, anyway, Megan," Travis was saying, quietly. "I'm still following the rodeo circuit."

"Oh, that's right!" she replied, unable to hide her obvious relief. "Well, that would work out okay." She went on, hopping up from the table. She began to pace. "I mean, we've got plenty of room," she said with an expansive wave of her arm. "Why, this old house rambles in all directions. There's several bedrooms..." She came to an abrupt halt, her voice trailing off. She eyed him uncertainly. "Would you expect to share my room?"

He took a deep breath and held it, his gaze never leaving hers. When he finally exhaled, he gave her a lopsided smile. "Whatever you're comfortable with, Megan."

"Oh." She thought about the idea of sharing a bedroom with Travis Kane and shivered. "Well, I'm certainly not comfortable with the thought of sharing my room with you...or anybody...really."

"I see."

She began to pace once again. "Well, I mean, the whole idea takes some getting used to, you've got to admit. I never expected to get married so I've never given it much thought."

"Why?"

She'd reached the window and was looking outside, wondering when the girls would be getting back from town, wondering how she could possibly explain to them what she was thinking about doing. She whirled around to face him, vaguely recalling his question. "Why what?" she repeated. "Why give it much thought? Because I've had other more important things to think about."

Travis stretched his long legs out straight, then tipped his chair back and crossed his ankles. "No, I want to know why you never thought you'd get married."

She threw her arms wide and grinned. "Who would be interested in marrying somebody like me who's trying to keep a run-down ranch going as well as raise a couple of sisters? Nobody in his right mind is going to be interested in getting involved in a situation like that." She eyed him speculatively.

"I am," he said mildly.

She continued to study him. Had she found the fly in this particular ointment? Had he fallen off a bull onto his head one too many times and scattered his brain cells? He appeared rational enough, but his suggestion had all the earmarks of a crazy man. However, he'd been smart enough to place a time condition on the agreement. She smiled at him as she reminded him. "Yes, but only for a year. Believe me, after a year you'll be more than ready to get away from this place." She nodded, seeing more and more advantages to his wild suggestion. "By that time Mollie will have graduated from high school. Who knows? Maybe both of them will want to move into town. Or maybe to Austin or San Antonio."

Suddenly feeling more lighthearted than she'd felt in weeks—no, more like months—Megan realized that she was starved. She went over to the refrigerator and opened the door. "Speaking of the girls, both of them stayed in town last night with friends. I don't know when they'll get home tonight, but I don't intend to hold supper for them. I'm hungry." She peered over her shoulder at him. "Do you want to stay and eat with me?"

He smiled and in a gentle voice, said, "I'd like that, Megan."

She began to rummage around inside the refrigerator. "It won't be anything fancy. Mollie's the real cook around here. I just throw together some of the basics and—"

She straightened and backed away from the refrigerator with her hands full, then turned to find Travis immediately behind her. He took the dishes out of her hands and placed them on the nearby counter, then reached behind her and closed the refrigerator door.

"I think we should seal the bargain, don't you?" he murmured, trapping her between him and the refrigerator.

Megan couldn't remember ever having been caught so off guard. Before she could think, his lips were pressing against hers. A bolt of electrical shock went through her. Travis was kissing her. Travis Kane. Kissing her. Her... Megan O'Brien... tomboy... the girl who...

Her thoughts scattered as her senses took over. She became aware of the woodsy scent of his after-shave, the minty flavor of his mouth, the muscled wall of his chest as it pressed against hers, his uneven breathing as he tilted his head to another angle, teasing her with his tongue. Her eyes drifted closed, savoring all the new and glorious sensations that were sweeping over her.

She'd never been kissed by a man before, a man whose hands were tracing her spine, shaping her buttocks and pulling her closer so that she could feel—could feel . . .

Megan's eyes flew open and she gave him a sudden shove. Caught off guard, he took a couple of quick steps back before regaining his balance.

They stared at each other, both of them breathing unevenly. Her heart felt as though it were going to leap out of her chest.

"It was just a kiss, Megan. That's all," he said quietly.

"Yeah, and Carlsbad Caverns is just a hole in the ground. That's all," she said, mimicking him.

"That's true," he replied, smiling.

She spun away and began to busy herself with making some sandwiches, doing her best to forget how she'd felt when Travis kissed her.

"I take it you don't want me to kiss you," he finally said in the silence that stretched between them.

She bit down on her lower lip, knowing that she couldn't lie to him, but not knowing exactly what the truth was. Continuing to keep busy with their meal, she said, "It isn't that. I— It's just that— I mean, I don't have a lot of experience in these things, and…" She couldn't think of how to continue.

He kept his distance from her when he said, "And you think that I mind? Just because you're innocent doesn't mean—"

She turned and glared at him. "I'm not innocent!" She closed her eyes and swallowed. Now she was *really* giving him the wrong idea about her! She opened her eyes and tried again. "I mean— What I *meant* was that anyone raised on a ranch knows all about reproduction and sex and— Well, you know what I mean. It's just that—" She waved her hand helplessly, not knowing how to explain how confused she was feeling at the moment.

He watched her intently. "Yeah, you've told me. You haven't done much dating. I understand."

She turned back to the counter, picked up the plate of sandwiches she'd prepared and carried it to the table. After refilling their glasses she motioned for him to sit down. "I don't know what you expect from me, that's all," she finally muttered, sitting down across from him and looking everywhere but at him.

He reached for a sandwich and put it on his plate. "I don't expect anything you don't want to give," he said in a careful tone of voice. "I realize that what I'm suggesting isn't the usual way of doing things."

"It's crazy, that's what it is. Who's going to believe it? It doesn't make any sense. I can't believe I'm actually considering it!" She took a big bite out of her sandwich, concentrating on eating and trying to distance herself from the familiar stranger across the table from her. How could she know somebody so well and yet not know him at all? How could she hate him—well, resent him anyway—for not noticing her when he was the big man on campus and she had so wanted him to see her as a young woman, and not the tomboy he'd pestered on the bus for years. She'd been invisible to him then. So why now? Why was this happening all these years later?

"I have a suggestion," he said, after finishing one of the sandwiches and reaching for another.

"What?" she asked suspiciously.

"I think we should keep the arrangement we've made just between the two of us. I think we'll both be more comfortable that way. Why don't we tell our families that we suddenly discovered our true feelings for each other and—"

"Nobody's going to believe that! Everybody knows that I— That is, that we—uh—"

"Yes?"

"What I mean is, we've never even been seen together."

"So maybe I've been writing you."

"The girls know better."

"Maybe I finally got up the nerve to confront you and admit how I feel about you."

She covered her mouth and began to laugh, shaking her head. "Oh, no. The girls would see right through that!"

"Not if you helped me."

"How?"

He watched her, his distinctive eyes glowing. "By pretending a little that you care for me, that we both want this."

"Your folks will—"

"I'll take care of my folks. You don't need to worry about them."

"Oh." She looked at the forgotten sandwich on her plate. She realized that although her stomach had been growling she was no longer hungry.

"When do you want to get married?"

She jerked her head up. "I—uh—"

"If you want to wait a while and let everyone get used to the idea, that's fine with me. An engagement would look more normal, anyway."

"You wouldn't mind?"

"I want you to be comfortable with the idea."

Her thoughts raced in all directions at once. "Well, if I'm going to make the mortgage payment on time—"

"You don't have to marry me before you get the money. I'll write you a check tonight that should cover it, plus whatever else you're going to need for a while."

"But I don't want you to think—"

"Don't worry about my thoughts, okay? Or my feelings. This is a straightforward business deal. I'm going to be going back out on the circuit next week and will be gone several weeks." He paused, thinking. "Maybe we should announce our engagement now. I'll get you a ring to wear, and we can start to plan the wedding. I assume you want to be married in the church."

"The church?" she squeaked. "But isn't that—I mean, for a business arrangement isn't that being a little—" She waved her hand helplessly.

"It's going to be a real marriage, Megan. Don't you think it needs to start out in the church?"

This must be the way Alice felt when she fell down the rabbit hole. "But knowing it's only going to be for a year makes it seem like a sham, somehow. I mean, if everybody's there to see us get married, aren't they going to wonder later why we decide to part?"

He washed the last bite of his third sandwich down with a long swallow of tea before replying. "In the first place, it's none of their business. In the second place, the way things are these days, more marriages than not end up that way."

She thought about that for a moment. "I suppose," she acknowledged.

"This way you'll have time to find a dress and decide what your sisters will wear."

All of this was coming too fast and furious for her. Her head was swimming. "A dress! Travis, I haven't worn a dress since my high school graduation!"

He grinned. "Well, maybe you can make an exception this one time. Of course if you feel more comfortable wearing your boots beneath it, go ahead."

Megan forced herself to eat her sandwich while Travis chatted on as though he planned weddings on a regular basis and there wasn't anything difficult about it. When she finished eating, he helped her clean up their dishes.

"Do you want me to be here when you tell the girls?" he asked, folding the dish towel he'd used and carefully hanging it on the rack.

"Uh, no," she said quickly, jolted by the mere thought. "No, I can tell them. I've just got to decide how to bring it up."

He folded his arms across his chest and leaned against the kitchen counter. "We could go to town tomorrow and look at rings."

She hid her hands behind her back. "Do you really think that's necessary?"

"Rings?" he asked, lifting his brow slightly. "Yes, I do."

"I mean, if we go into Agua Verde to look for rings, everybody in town will know about it within the hour."

He grinned, reminding her of the mischievous boy he'd once been. Not a good omen at all, in her mind. "Well, that's one way of getting the news out."

She dropped her gaze to the floor, feeling horribly out of her element. She had no problem discussing anything at all about the ranch or the girls, but rings? Weddings? Marriage? She'd never given them a thought.

"Or... we could drive into Austin, if you like. We could make a day of it, maybe see a show. You know, make an occasion of it. Surely you can stay out late for one night."

She looked up and caught his intent gaze. "Why are you doing this, Travis? I don't understand. Why are you willing to tie yourself up in such a fashion? Surely you've met women during your travels that—''

"None that I'd marry."

"But still—''

"I always intended to marry a hometown girl, didn't you know?" he said, grinning once again.

"Then why didn't you marry Carrie Schwarz? You dated her most of your senior year."

He looked startled. "Carrie? Isn't she married?"

"She is now, but she waited for you for years."

He laughed. "I doubt that."

"No. She did. She went away to college, but came home as often as she could, hoping to find you here. She found out during the Christmas holidays that first year that you were seeing Trish Kronig whenever you were in town."

"You sure have a memory for names. I'd forgotten both of those girls."

She walked back to the window and looked outside. It was dark. The yard light near the barn gave off a faint glow. "I'm sure they haven't forgotten you," she said quietly, reminding herself how easily a heart could be broken. Hadn't she congratulated herself for not being pretty enough to get his attention back then? Hadn't she considered herself lucky that she'd never gone through what those girls had? Where was her sane, sensible self *now*, when she really needed her?

He picked up his hat. "All that was years ago, Megan. I was just a kid back then."

She turned to face him. "But now you're all grown-up, huh?"

He flashed his devastating smile, his eyes sparkling. "God! I hope so, since I'm making plans to get married and settle down."

"But you aren't giving up the rodeo," she said pointedly.

"Well, no, not yet. I only have a few years to ride. The rodeo makes an old man out of you real quick."

"Or kills you."

He settled his hat on his head. "Not me. I'm too mean and too tough to die." He opened the screen door and stepped out onto the porch. "I'll pick you up right after lunch tomorrow, if that's okay with you?"

She paused for a moment. Now was the time to back out, if she was going to. Unfortunately she had a sinking feeling in her stomach that she was actually going to go through with this completely insane idea. Her options were limited. She'd prayed for a way to save the ranch and she'd been given one. The irony of her situation flooded over her.

She crossed her arms, hugging them against her. "All right, Travis. I'll be ready," she finally replied, silently acknowledging to herself that in all of her life she'd never made such a frightening decision. She and the girls wouldn't lose the ranch, but marrying Travis Kane could end up costing her even more than her home in the long run.

Keeping her distance from him had protected her as a young girl. What could she use as protection now?

Three

Megan took a long, soaking bath after Travis left, trying to come to terms with what she had agreed to do. Eventually she got out and dried off, putting on her faded nightshirt and worn bathrobe, but she was too restless to go to sleep. Instead she curled up on the couch to watch television and wait for the girls to come home.

She was still on the couch, dozing, when she heard the family pickup truck coming up the lane. The thing rattled and roared, sounding more like a threshing machine than a vehicle for transportation.

She'd let Mollie take it into town last night, since both Mollie and Maribeth had wanted to spend the night with friends. They never complained about living twenty-five miles from town, but were always eager to go into town to visit their friends, or hang out at the local hamburger haven.

The girls didn't complain about anything. She'd fought so hard to keep them when the county officials first suggested they might be placed in foster homes. She'd insisted that she could look after them and that with Butch's help she could also run the ranch. After all, she'd been following her daddy around that ranch from the time she could walk. He'd have her sitting in the saddle in front of him on the back of his favorite mount or riding next to him in that old pickup.

She should have been a boy, but her dad never seemed to mind that he had girls. She remembered how he used to laugh when the other ranchers in the coffee shop would mention his harem.

There were times, like today, when the ache of missing her mom and dad was so painful she thought she might die from it. Maybe according to the calendar she was twenty-four years old, but she didn't feel as if she'd ever gotten past sixteen when it came to knowing about men and how to socialize. In a few short hours her youthful teenage years had abruptly ended with the news that both parents had been killed in a fiery car crash outside of Fort Worth. Practically overnight she'd had to become both mom and dad to Mollie and Maribeth, as well as in charge of the Circle B Ranch. She'd had to become an adult in order to deal with all the officials who'd tried to separate the three of them. She'd fought hard to keep them all together—and she'd won. Tonight she'd made another decision to ensure her sisters' continued well-being. Her peace of mind was a very small sacrifice to make to protect them.

The kitchen screen door squeaked as one of the girls opened it. Megan could hear Maribeth chattering away. She smiled. Maribeth was such a live wire. Whatever thought crossed her mind popped out of her mouth. She seemed to run through life with her arms flung open wide, ready to embrace the world and everything in it.

She wore her bright red hair streaming over her shoulders and down her back, pulled away from her face by a large hair clip. Her wide brown eyes were her most expressive feature, mirroring her every thought.

Maribeth had been eight when their parents had died.

Although Mollie was two years older than Maribeth, Megan thought of Mollie as being almost as old as she was. Maybe it was because she was the quiet one in the family. She'd always been close to Mama. After Mama died, Mollie seemed to become less talkative than ever.

She was good in the house, keeping the place clean, cooking their meals while she still kept up her schoolwork.

Mollie was so bright. She deserved the chance to go on to college. Megan had tried so hard to put money away for Mollie's education but there had never been enough to stretch. Mollie would be graduating from high school in a few short weeks. She'd already found a job clerking in one of the stores in town, but Mollie deserved so much more in life.

She was the real beauty in the family, with her creamy white skin and dark, auburn hair. Her eyes looked too blue to be real, as if she wore tinted contacts. She never seemed to be aware of her looks and was the only one in town who was surprised when she'd been named homecoming queen the previous fall.

"Hi, Megan!" Maribeth said, bouncing into the room. "What are you doing up? You're usually sacked out in bed by this time of night." Maribeth threw herself into the big overstuffed chair across from Megan.

Megan made a face and grinned. "You make me sound like an ol' grandma. I've been known to stay up past nine o'clock on occasions."

Mollie paused in the doorway. "You want something to drink? I bought a six-pack of soda."

She glanced around, still smiling. "Mmm. Sounds good."

"You'll never guess who I saw in town today!" Maribeth announced dramatically, her eyes wide.

"Probably not," Megan drawled. "So why don't you tell me?"

"Travis Kane! I couldn't believe it. Me and Bobby and Chris went to the post office for Bobby's mom, and who should be walking out of the post office but Travis Kane, himself. You should have seen Bobby! He's always dreamed of being able to ride wild bulls as well as Travis, not to mention his skill with calf roping. He was practically stuttering when Travis spoke to us."

Mollie walked back in with three large glasses filled with ice cubes and soda. She offered one to Megan, who took one, then Mollie handed another to Maribeth.

"I know. Travis came out here today."

Mollie looked around at her in surprise. "Travis Kane came out here? What in the world for?"

Instead of answering her, Megan looked at Maribeth. "Just what did you tell Travis about us, Maribeth?"

At least her youngest sister had the decency to blush. "Well, nothing, really. He was just asking about you and all and I told him— Well, I guess I may have mentioned that you were making yourself sick worrying about us maybe going to lose the ranch."

Mollie sank down at the other end of the couch and stared at Maribeth. "Maribeth! You didn't! You can't go around telling everybody our business like that!"

"I wasn't. Everybody already knows everything about us, anyway. It's no secret that we're probably going to lose the ranch. So what's the big deal?"

Mollie shook her head in disgust. "Well, you don't go around blabbing everything you know," she replied.

Megan dropped her head back against the couch. "Oh, yes she does!" she said with a sigh.

"Well, he was asking about you and I was just trying to be polite and—"

"More than likely, you were trying to hold his attention just a little longer," Mollie said. "You and Bobby would be charter members of his fan club if he had one."

Maribeth swung her legs over the side of the chair. "Hey! That's a great idea. Maybe we can start—"

"I was just joking," Mollie said hastily. "Travis Kane certainly doesn't need a fan club! His ego's already big enough as it is."

"You can say that again," Megan muttered.

Maribeth stuck her bottom lip out. "I don't know why y'all have to be so hateful about Travis. What has he ever done to make you both sneer at him so much?"

Megan shifted, pulling her knees up and resting her chin on them. She wasn't comfortable with the turn in the conversation but she couldn't think of any way to change the subject that wouldn't be too obvious.

She was surprised when Mollie answered. She had seldom heard Mollie so vocal. "Because he thinks he's God's gift to women, that's why. Always swaggering around in those tight jeans he wears, with his hat brim pulled down low over those fancy mirror sunglasses of his, giving all the girls that drop-dead gorgeous smile so they'll swoon at his feet. I think he's perfectly disgusting."

Megan's heart seemed to sink in her chest. "I had no idea you disliked him so," Megan said quietly.

Mollie glanced around at her in surprise. "Well, you've never had much good to say about him, yourself! I remember when you were both in school, you used to come home complaining about him and calling him all kinds of names. Mama used to laugh at how mad you got at him, remember?''

''I was just a kid. He used to delight in teasing me on the school bus to and from school. Since it was almost an hour to get to town, he had plenty of time to think of ways to torment me.''

''Well,'' Mollie replied, her cheeks flushed with color, ''my friend Betsy told me about how he flirted with her older sister, carrying on until her sister fell in love with him, then he just dropped her like that, like she was nothing to him. He's broken a lot of hearts in this county. I think he should go away and stay away!''

''Well, *I* think he's definitely hunk-of-the-month material, myself,'' Maribeth announced. ''Just because you two don't ever have any boyfriends doesn't mean you shouldn't appreciate a good-looking specimen like Travis when you get the chance. Bobby says—''

Megan just shook her head. ''Here we go again. If Bobby says it, it must be gospel, right?''

''Well, he knows rodeos. He and his dad are always going to them. He's seen Travis compete and says he's totally awesome. That's why he was named World Champion last year.''

Megan uncurled herself from the couch and stood. ''Well, I think I'm going to take myself off to bed. You're really making me feel my years, Maribeth,'' she said, ruffling her sister's long wavy hair. ''I take it you had a good time in town.''

''Oh, yeah. Rita's a lot of fun. Her mom said to tell you that anytime I want to spend the night in town, that I can stay with them.''

''Well, I'm glad to hear you didn't totally wear out your welcome.''

She glanced at Mollie, caught her eye and nodded toward the hallway. "I'll see y'all in the morning."

Megan climbed the stairs to her bedroom. She hoped Mollie recognized her signal. She wasn't going to be able to sleep tonight until she talked to her and tried to explain.

She hadn't realized Mollie's feelings toward Travis were so strong or so negative. Megan knew that she had herself to blame for some of that. She'd never kept her disdain for Travis hidden from Mollie or anyone else around home. Now she was going to be forced to provide some kind of explanation for the change in her attitude—without giving the real one. If Travis preferred people not to know the truth, she owed him that much.

She slipped out of her robe and sank onto the side of her bed. What a mess. It had all seemed so logical and businesslike when Travis first made his suggestion. A year's marriage; a limited partnership agreement. A business deal. She would be his wife in exchange for help with the ranch. Wasn't that reasonable enough?

She doubted that Mollie would see it that way. As protective as Mollie was, she'd probably think that Megan was in love with him or something. She'd probably think she was having her heart broken when that wouldn't be the case, at all.

Megan heard a soft tap on her door. She smiled and softly said, "Come on in."

Mollie opened the door and slipped inside. "You wanted to see me?"

"Yeah." She patted the bed and Mollie sat down beside her. "There's something I need to talk to you about that I would just as soon not discuss in front of Maribeth. At least, not yet."

"I can certainly understand that. Telling Maribeth anything is like putting it on the six o'clock news!"

"I need to ask a favor of you."

"Sure. Anything."

Megan smiled and shook her head in amusement. "You don't know what the favor is."

"Doesn't matter."

Impulsively Megan leaned over and hugged Mollie. "Have I ever told you how much I love and appreciate you? I couldn't have made it this far without you."

Mollie's cheeks pinkened. "Don't be silly. You make it sound like you're on your deathbed or something. So... what gives? What's the favor?"

Megan took a deep breath, feeling very uncomfortable. She let the air out of her lungs in a gusty sigh. "I was wondering if I could borrow one of your dresses tomorrow."

Mollie stared at her in shock, as though unable to credit what she was hearing. "A dress?" she repeated. "You want to borrow one of my dresses?"

"Isn't that just what I said?"

"I was sure my hearing had suddenly gone on the blink. You never wear dresses. Why do you need one now?"

"It's a long story."

Mollie slid up further on the bed and folded her legs, lotus-fashion. "Well, I don't care how long it is, this is one story I've gotta hear!"

Megan scooted back on the bed as well, leaning against the headboard, resigned to facing Mollie's reaction. "I'm going with Travis Kane to Austin tomorrow."

"You mean, on a date?"

"Um-hmm."

"But you never date."

"I know."

"You haven't dated anyone since high school."

"I know."

"You never wear dresses."

"You've already pointed that out, Mollie! I know I never wear them, which is why I'm asking to borrow one of yours. We're close to the same size. I'm probably no more than an inch shorter than you. It won't really matter what it looks like on me." She shoved her hand through her hair. "I know I'll look silly, but I wanted to appear more—" she waved her hand in a circle "—you know, more feminine."

Mollie's smile was filled with amused affection. "You couldn't help looking feminine if you tried, Megan."

"Huh! You've got to be kidding. With my bobbed hair and in my coveralls more than one stranger has thought I was a boy!"

"Only if the stranger was blind. You have a very feminine face, a long slender—almost regal looking—neck, a graceful way of moving, and a beautifully shaped body."

"Now I know you're crazy! Me? I'm too skinny. I'm—"

"You're small-boned and delicate looking...not skinny. I think we could maybe trim your hair a little, find one of my dresses that you'd like as well as be comfortable in, and perhaps try a little makeup on you."

"I've never worn makeup in my life."

"So? If you're going to change your habits by wearing a dress, you might as well go whole hog and do it all."

Megan hesitantly touched her hair. "I don't know what to do with it. I just whack it off when it starts getting in my eyes. You've always been the one who trims the back for me."

"Teresa at the beauty shop in town has been teaching me how to cut hair when she didn't have any customers. It's not all that hard. She gave me some scissors and things. I think I could do something really cute with your hair." She, too, ran her fingers through Megan's hair. "It's so thick and curly."

Megan scowled. "Looks like a mop."

Mollie grinned. "Once it's shaped, I think it'll look fine."

"Whatever you think," Megan replied, sighing. "I'm going to put myself in your hands on this one."

Mollie slipped off the bed. "Okay, we'll look through my closet in the morning, and I'll do your hair. It shouldn't take long. When is he coming?"

"About one o'clock."

Mollie paused in the doorway of the bedroom and said, "I don't understand. Why, after years of not dating, would you suddenly decide to accept a date with Travis Kane, of all people?"

Megan tried to think of something to say that would prepare Mollie for what was going to happen, but her mind remained blank. After a moment, she shrugged and lamely offered, "He isn't that bad, Mollie."

Mollie snorted. "Hah! He's arrogant, he's egotistical, and he's irresponsible. And that, my dear sister, is a direct quote from you the last time he happened to be mentioned in a conversation. Exactly when did he redeem himself in your estimation?"

Megan clasped her hands in her lap, carefully studying them. "He's offered to help us out until we can get back on our feet. He doesn't want us to lose the ranch."

Mollie leaned against the doorjamb, folding her arms. "I find that a little hard to believe. What's in it for him?"

Megan avoided Mollie's gaze. "He says he just wants to help, since we've known each other for so long and we're neighbors and all."

"Uh-huh. And then he asks you for a date. What exactly is the catch here? There's got to be a few strings attached. I'm sure Maribeth fed him all the details about our situation. No doubt he knows there's no way we have the money to pay back any loan he might make to us."

So there it was. There was no way she could avoid telling Mollie the truth. She clasped her hands tightly in her lap and looked up at Mollie, who continued to steadily watch her from across the room. "He asked me to marry him."

"What?" Mollie shouted, leaping away from the doorway and over to the bed as if she'd been shot out of a cannon.

"Shhhh! Don't let Maribeth hear you."

Mollie clasped both hands over her mouth and began to pace jerkily up and down the room. Megan closed her eyes. This wasn't going well at all, but then, what had she expected, given the circumstances and the long-standing feud she'd carried on—albeit a trifle one-sided—with Travis.

Mollie finally paused long enough beside Megan to hiss, "The nerve of the man! Thinking that you would even consider selling yourself like some—"

"Mollie, I told him I would," Megan said quietly.

Mollie looked as though she'd been slapped across the face. She'd been leaning over the bed when Megan gave her the news of what she'd done. Mollie's blue eyes slowly widened, larger and larger, as though she was seeing a specter slowly rising from the grave. "Oh, Megan, no," she whispered, scarcely breathing. "Please no. You mustn't do this. I know you've been worrying about what's going to happen to us, but nothing is worth your sacrificing your happiness like this." Tears began to fill her eyes.

Megan scrambled off the bed and threw her arms around her sister. "Oh, Mollie...it's okay. Really it is. We're treating it like a business arrangement. He won't even be around all that much. He's going to be on the rodeo circuit, traveling for most of the year. You know the circuit runs from January to December and he has to enter as many as he can to get the points he needs. Why, we'll seldom see him."

She leaned back so that she could see Mollie's stricken face. She grabbed a handful of tissues and patted Mollie's cheeks. "I couldn't accept a loan from him, Mollie. I didn't want to be obligated to him."

"Megan! What in the world do you consider marriage to be, if it isn't an obligation?"

"A partnership," she hastily replied. "That's what we're forming . . . a partnership. He says it's time for him to settle down. He says he wants a home. He says—"

"Oh, Megan, honey," Mollie said, shaking her head. "Travis Kane is going to break your heart."

Megan tilted her chin slightly. "Not unless I let him."

"You may not have a choice."

Megan dropped her arms and moved away from the bed and her sister. She walked over to her dresser and picked up a comb. Absently playing with it, she said, "We always have choices, Mollie. Remember that. Both Travis and I know and understand what we're doing and why we're doing it. It'll be okay, I promise. Please don't worry about me. I'm a big girl now." *I would do this—and more—to take care of you and Maribeth,* she added silently.

Mollie just shook her head. "I know. You've been like a parent to us for so long," she replied, as though reading Megan's thoughts. "But in some ways you're still so young and so naive. I swear, if that bastard ever tries to—"

"Mollie! I've never known you to use such language." Megan stared at her in disbelief.

"I've never watched my sister sell herself to the highest bidder, either," she blurted out before Megan's shocked look registered. Mollie hurried over to her, hugging her older sister. "I'm sorry, Megan! I'm so sorry. I didn't really mean that. It's just that you've made so many sacrifices for us already that it breaks my heart to see you throwing yourself away on someone who isn't worth it."

Megan hugged her back before she said, "You know, Mollie, I think that maybe we've both been too quick to judge Travis. Let's face it, if he was really as irresponsible as we think, he would never have made such an offer in the first place. Besides, look at it this way. I'm twenty-four years old. I've never dated anyone. I've never socialized. I never—ever—thought that I might get married someday. And now, all of that is going to change. Maybe, for the very first time in my life, I've got the chance to have what other women take for granted—a man who cares about me, who's willing to help me with my responsibilities. It's not as if we're total strangers, after all. Our families have been friends and neighbors for years and years." She went back to the bed and sat down. "I want to give him a chance, Mollie. I think I owe him that much, just for his willingness to help us out. I also want the ranch to have a chance to survive as the Circle B. Please trust me to know what I'm doing. Please?"

Mollie walked over and gave her a quick kiss on the cheek. "You're worn-out, Megan. I should have seen that before. Get some sleep now. Just because he made the offer doesn't mean you have to take him up on it. Let's just treat tomorrow as a chance for you to go out and have some fun for a change." She turned off the lamp beside the bed. "We'll work on getting you dolled up in the morning. Ol' Travis won't know what hit him when he gets a look at you all fixed up. He won't believe his good luck at getting the chance to take you out for the day!" She turned and left the room, quietly closing the door behind her.

Megan sat there in the darkened room, staring toward the door for a long time before she got into bed. She pulled the covers up around her shoulders and stared at the ceiling, wishing she knew if she was doing the right thing. Mollie's arguments were valid and she knew it. Megan knew she was way over her head on this one. What if she was wrong?

She'd sounded so sure of herself, asking Mollie to trust her judgment. What a fraud she was.

She had no idea if she was doing the right thing. The only thing she knew was that she had to try to save the family's legacy. She had to do whatever she could, no matter how painful or uncertain the future appeared.

Marrying Travis Kane seemed to be the only answer.

Four

Travis turned off the county road onto the lane leading to the ranch buildings of the Circle B. His dad's ranch entrance was a little over five miles down the road from here. The O'Brien house could be seen from the road, sitting on a rise overlooking the surrounding countryside. The two-story building had an old-world grace reminiscent of a much earlier era, its stone walls decorated with wooden filigree and curlicues around the veranda, which circled the lower floor and provided shade from the hot Texas sunshine.

The house where he'd grown up didn't look all that different. Many of the ranches in this area had been established more than a hundred years ago, handed down from one generation to the next in keeping with family tradition.

The closer he got, the more he could see the signs of neglect and decay around the aging dwelling. One of the front porch steps looked rotted through and would probably be a hazard to anyone unsuspecting enough to approach the often ignored front entrance of the house.

Nobody living in these parts used front doors to a house, anyway, which was probably why Megan hadn't attempted to make an unessential repair.

His knowledgeable gaze noted that all the fences he could see were in good working order, as were all the outbuildings such as the barn and shed located a short distance from the house. Like most ranchers, Megan had neglected the house in favor of keeping the ranch property itself in repair.

Travis pulled up beside the low stone fence that separated the house and its neglected lawn from the rest of the ranch yard. From the corner of his eye he caught the slight flutter of a curtain in one of the upstairs windows. Somebody knew he'd arrived.

He'd been awake since before dawn this morning, thinking about the day ahead. He more than half expected Megan to greet him with the news that she'd changed her mind about going to Austin with him, much less marrying him.

If she wasn't the most unworldly person he knew, she was certainly high on the list.

Did she honestly believe that the only reason he had offered to marry her was so that she would accept his help to save the ranch? Could she possibly be so blind to her many wonderful qualities, to her attractiveness, to her adorable traits that she didn't recognize the way he felt about her, the way he had always felt about her?

Travis couldn't remember how old he'd been when he first faced the realization that he loved Megan O'Brien, but it must have been while they were still in grade school. He'd been a typical show-off male back then, vying for her attention by dropping pebbles down the back of her shirt, grabbing her pigtails and treating them like reins of a horse, and teasing her unmercifully at every opportunity.

Hadn't she known, even then, that little boys signal their devotion in such a way? He sighed. She sure didn't know much about the male animal, that's for sure. Everybody else in the county had known what his behavior meant. He'd gotten a lot of teasing, which was why he'd backed off by the time he reached high school. She'd had little use for him by then and made her opinion of him quite clear, snubbing him, ignoring him. His adolescent ego had taken a real beating and he hadn't wanted to place himself in a position to be rejected by her back then.

Instead he'd gone out of his way to excel in sports and in the classroom in hopes of impressing her with his abilities. Even his rodeoing had been an attempt to show her what he could do.

As soon as Maribeth had told him what a struggle she was having, he'd immediately wanted to leap upon his dazzling white charger and come dashing to her rescue. His concern had been enough to overcome her last rejection of him when he'd come home a couple of years ago, flush with success, and had dared to invite her out on a date. She'd turned him down.

Well, now he had that date...finally...after all these years.

He'd scarcely slept the night before, his mind racing with thoughts about today. They were going to spend several hours together for the very first time as adults. He was no longer that silly kid with a crush. He was now a grown man with a deep abiding love for a woman who could barely tolerate him. However, she had agreed to marry him. Wasn't that a start?

The hardest part for him was to remember not to show too much interest in her. He kept reminding himself that he had to remain casual and offhand toward her. The family friend role, that's what he had to concentrate on. Man oh man, that was going to take some real concentration on his part. He'd spent most of his life comparing every girl he met—then all the women he'd met—to Megan O'Brien. None of them had been able to measure up.

He'd never forget that time back when he'd been a senior in high school and captain of the football team. The team was doing great that fall and he'd been looking really good on the playing field. All of that had finally given him enough confidence...finally...to get up the nerve to ask her to the homecoming dance.

At sixteen, she wasn't dating anyone. He'd made it his business to find out for sure. Her folks had always been very strict with her, and he hadn't been sure exactly how to go about asking—whether or not to discuss it with her father first in order to convince him that she would be perfectly safe going out with him and that he would treat her with respect and care.

Before he could get up his nerve for that particular hurdle to his hopeful plans, her parents had been killed in that god-awful car crash. She'd missed several weeks of school after that and, even when she'd returned, he'd known she wouldn't be interested in anything he could say to her.

All of that was years ago, though. They'd both grown up. They'd both survived. Now, here he was once again determined to win his fair lady, even if she thought it was merely a business offer.

He had a year to convince her to make it a permanent merger.

He glanced up at that window again, trying not to think too much about the possibility that she might have already changed her mind.

Travis slowly opened the truck door and stepped out of the truck cab, tugging his hat low over his sunshades.

"Howdy, Travis," Butch called from where he stood between the wide opening of the barn. "You lost or somethin'? What brings you back out here today?"

Travis briefly glanced at the house before sauntering over to where Butch stood watching him. Facing Megan once again would come soon enough. He wasn't in any hurry if she had bad news to tell him. If the news was good, she'd be spending the rest of the day with him, anyway.

"It's nice to see you again, Butch. How're things going with you?" he offered, holding out his hand. The men shook hands.

"Can't complain. I been hearin' some good things about you, son. You been winnin' some pretty fancy titles on the circuit, I hear."

"Yeah." Travis grinned. "It's been a hoot, all right."

"Kinda dangerous profession, though. I mean, it's okay to go to some of these regional affairs, but doing it all the time can get kinda rough, can't it?"

Travis nodded. "Yeah. It's definitely a young man's sport. I figure I'll have to quit by the time I'm thirty or so. That gives me another three or four years."

"When are you going out on the road again?"

Travis glanced at the house before answering. "Probably next week."

"So what brings you out here today?"

"I'm taking Megan to Austin for the afternoon and evening."

Butch shoved his hat to the back of his head and scratched his temple. "The hell you are! Did she agree to go?"

"Um, yes," Travis mumbled, looking down at the pointed toes of his boots. "Yes, she did."

Butch grinned broadly. "Well, I'll be hornswoggled. That's good news. That girl never does get away from this place. You know, now that you mention it, she didn't come outside this morning. I didn't give it much thought...figured she'd finally decided to rest up a little. Looks to me like she decided to take the whole day off."

Travis glanced toward the house. "Guess I'd better go see if she's ready."

"Well, y'all have fun today."

"Thanks, Butch. See you later."

From her position behind the sheer curtains of her bedroom, Megan watched Travis walk away from Butch in his loose-limbed saunter toward the back entrance of the house. She shivered. What had caused her to toss out all her long-held beliefs about this man and decide to accept his unorthodox offer of marriage?

Travis Kane was a law unto himself. She was the first to admit that he'd always made her jumpy and nervous. What if she couldn't get over the way she reacted around him?

Mollie's blunt comments last night had shaken her more than she had expected. Mollie was right. Megan had never had anything good to say about him. Her decision to marry him made no sense whatsoever.

She'd lain awake last night, thinking about refusing him. She could do that. Nobody was forcing her into anything. She could go to the bank, tell the banker she couldn't make the payment. She could let them foreclose on the ranch. And sometime in the future, after they'd lost everything, she could remind herself that if she'd just had a little more courage, she might have made a different choice. She might have found herself married and still living on the family ranch.

Travis suddenly glanced up at her window and she hastily took a step backward, not wanting him to know that she was still lurking in her room, uncomfortable about going downstairs and facing her world dressed the way she was.

Megan turned nervously toward the oval mirror in the corner and stared at her image. She was forced to admit that the dress she wore fit her surprisingly well . . . as did the sandals with the tiny stacked heels. The problem was that she didn't look like herself. Peering more closely into the mirror, she studied her face and hair.

She was still amazed at how successfully Mollie had trimmed her thick hair. She had thinned and shaped it around her face and ears, calling attention to her eyes. She didn't remember them ever looking quite so large or so blue. She always thought of them as blueish gray, but now they sparkled like blue topaz.

Megan wasn't used to seeing herself in makeup. Mollie had darkened her lashes and brows slightly, added touches of color around her eyes and across her cheekbones, and finished with a soft pink lipstick that made her mouth look slightly pouty.

"Megan," Mollie called from downstairs. "Travis's here."

The cool tone made Megan wince. She knew she'd better hurry down before Mollie made her dislike toward him obvious. For a quiet person, Mollie certainly had strong opinions and, for some reason these past two days, she wasn't having any difficulty expressing them.

Travis had already noticed a definite chill in the air as soon as Mollie came to the door in response to his light tap on the screen. Without a word she opened the door, then turned away and called out to Megan without greeting him.

"How've you been, Mollie? I haven't seen you in quite a while."

Mollie went back to mixing and stirring something on the counter. From the looks and smell of things, she was in the midst of some heavy-duty, mouth-watering baking.

Without looking around at him, she said, "Fine," in a short tone of voice.

He glanced around the large kitchen, recognizing the place as the hub of the home. He looked back at her, but she was studiously ignoring him. He slowly removed his hat and held the brim in both hands, turning it.

"Have you finished school yet?"

"This is my last year."

"Where do you intend to go to college?"

Her glance held a hint of contempt. "We don't have the money for college."

"Did you try for any scholarships?"

"No. Megan needs me here."

There was a slight sound at the doorway into the hall and he looked around. He froze at the sight of Megan standing there, her manner more hesitant than he'd ever seen her.

She wore a lemon-colored sundress that lovingly cupped her breasts and waist, then flared into a full skirt that ended at her knees. He caught himself staring at her curving calves and slender ankles before his gaze ended on her pink-painted toenails in strappy sandals.

He swallowed hard, his gaze bouncing back over the unfamiliar sight of her bare legs and shoulders. Shoestring-size straps were the only things holding the dress in place.

When his eyes finally met hers Travis forced himself to nod. His throat felt dry. He couldn't get over the change from the coverall-covered woman of the day before. Even her face looked different. Softer, somehow. Her eyes were definitely wary. Even her hair looked smoother, silkier, somehow.

Travis could feel his heart racing and he battled for control, determined not to reveal his stunned reaction to this new look Megan had chosen.

"Hi, Megan," he said, his voice sounding gruff and raspy to his own ears. He cleared his throat. "You look very nice."

She came toward him, only her eyes betraying her unease. "Thank you." She looked past him and he turned. Mollie was watching them, her displeasure obvious. "I don't know when I'll be home," Megan was saying, "so don't worry if it's late."

Mollie gave her a brief nod and returned her attention to her dough. "Be careful" was all she said.

Megan hurried past him, pausing on the porch to wait for him to join her. It didn't take a rocket scientist to figure out there was something obviously wrong between the two sisters, Travis thought, as he followed Megan outside.

She kept at least two arm's length distance between them as she ran down the steps.

"Well, look-ee here," Butch hollered, striding across the open space between the barn and the house. "I almost didn't recognize you, missy."

Travis thought he heard a sound suspiciously like a groan from Megan.

"I'd look a little foolish working around here in a getup like this, now, wouldn't I?" she replied a little tartly.

Butch laughed. "That's for sure. I'm so used to seeing you in those shapeless coveralls I'd almost forgot what a good-lookin' gal you are," he said, his admiration evident. "Those sure are show-girl legs hidin' beneath all the denim."

"Butch!" Her face had turned as rosy as her nail polish. "Cut it out!"

Travis laughed. He couldn't help enjoying the interplay between the two of them. Stepping around her, he opened the passenger side of the truck and helped her inside. He was able to enjoy the flash of exposed legs as she took the step up into the cab. He closed the door, then turned around and winked at the older man. "Never underestimate the O'Brien women, Butch," he warned. "They're just full of surprises."

"You take good care of her now, you hear?" Butch said, straightening to his full height. "Just because she doesn't have no daddy to look after her doesn't mean—"

"I know, Butch. I promise to take very good care of her and not let her come to any harm."

Megan rested her arm on the open window and leaned out. "I'll probably be late getting back home since we're going to Austin, Butch. I don't want you waiting up with your shotgun, you hear me?" she warned.

Butch looked sheepish and nodded.

"I'm a grown woman and I can take care of myself," she added for good measure.

"You're no bigger'n a minute and you know it," he muttered, half under his breath.

Travis clapped him on the back and in a low voice said, "I'll keep her safe. Count on it."

They drove away from the house and down the lane. Megan leaned forward and looked out the side mirror. "I can't figure out what's got into Butch today. He's acting like you've kidnapped me and plan to sell me into white slavery."

"Can't say that I blame him," he drawled, glancing at her out of the corner of his eye. "You're looking mighty good... pretty near irresistible, if you ask me." He had the pleasure of watching her turn rosy once again.

"I should have worn jeans, I suppose. I never dreamed that putting on a dress would cause such a stir," she muttered half under her breath.

"I'm sorry, Megan," he said, reaching over and taking her hand. She stiffened, but didn't try to pull away. "I find it too easy to tease you, I suppose," he admitted. "I guess it's because you respond so easy to teasing."

Encouraged by the fact that she hadn't jerked her hand back and socked him—which he knew she was perfectly capable of doing—he slipped his fingers between hers and rested their clasped hands on his thigh.

"I take it from her attitude that you told Mollie about our plans and that she's a tad less than thrilled to have me as a brother-in-law."

He could feel her body tense all the way to her fingertips. "She just doesn't want me hurt."

He glanced at her in surprise. "And she thinks I would hurt you in some way?"

She smoothed her skirt with her free hand. "She's just a little protective, that's all. We've always been close, especially since the folks died."

"What's Mollie got against me, if I may ask?"

She sighed. "Your reputation, mostly."

He frowned. "I wasn't aware I had one."

He could feel her gaze on him. "C'mon, Travis. This is me you're talking to. Don't be so modest."

"I don't know what you're talking about."

She shook her head. "I suppose you're going to deny that you're known as a heartbreaker around these parts—that love 'em and leave 'em seems to be your personal creed?"

"*What?!*" The truck swerved and he let go of her hand to place both hands on the wheel. He hadn't wanted his reaction to her words to show, but he knew he was too late to hide it.

"What did you expect would be said about you when you've stopped seeing everyone you ever dated the minute she got serious about you?"

He rubbed the frown that had formed over the bridge of his nose. "What was I supposed to do? Anytime somebody started talking about the future or an engagement or about having a family I knew it was time to stop seeing her."

"Exactly."

He gave her a quick glance of surprise. "And that was wrong? Since I had no intention of marrying anyone it seems to me I did the honorable thing. I never led anyone on, or promised them anything. I never took advantage of anyone...."

"Just walked away and left them with their hearts broken. Yes, I know."

He gripped the steering wheel a little tighter. "But this is crazy, Megan. How can I be responsible for how somebody else feels? I don't have any control over that."

"I know."

"I dated women whose company I enjoyed. We had fun together. I liked them, but I never told a one of them that I loved them."

"So?"

"Lying would have—"

"Nobody's talking about lying." She didn't say anything else for several minutes and he was too astonished to think of anything more to add to the conversation. When she finally spoke again, she said, "I suppose Mollie's concerned about your motive. Why would anybody believe that Travis Kane—the guy who's run from any kind of commitment for all these years—would suddenly show up out of the blue and offer to marry me, even if it's only a business arrangement? Mollie's concerns make perfect sense to me. Of course, the way I look at it, marriage can work for your benefit, too. I mean, if you don't want to be hounded all the time by women wanting to marry you, then marrying me is a solution of sorts." She glanced over at him. "At least it'll give you a few months' breathing space."

"I'm not believin' this conversation," he muttered under his breath.

"What did you say?"

"I was just wondering if you're gettin' hungry. I skipped lunch today—" there was no use admitting he'd been too nervous to eat "—so I thought I might stop somewhere along the way and get something."

"Okay by me."

He glanced at her out of the corner of his eye. "You hungry?"

"Not particularly."

"Then we can wait until we get to Austin."

"Don't be silly! I can always have something to drink while you have a hamburger or something. What's the matter with you today?" She leaned forward so she could see more of his face. "You've been acting kind of strange."

"I'm feeling kind of strange," he admitted, hoping that eating would be a cure of sorts.

They passed into the outside limits of a small town and Travis saw a fast-food place up ahead. He pulled in and gave them an order that included a drink for each of them.

They were pulling back onto the highway when Megan asked, "So, are you going to tell me what's bothering you?" She unwrapped his burger and handed it to him, then scooted closer to him and held out his fries so that he could reach them.

Rather than answer her, he took a big bite of the burger and thoughtfully chewed, deciding what he was going to say to her. After taking a drink, he cleared his throat and said, "I thought maybe that you'd change your mind." There. He'd admitted it out loud.

"I thought about it."

He continued to eat his meal in the silence of the truck's cab. "And?" he asked when she didn't say anything more.

She gave a tiny shrug and sighed. "I decided that since you were willing to help us out by going to such an extreme as to marry me, I would accept your offer in the spirit you meant it. At least you didn't talk a lot of nonsense about being in love with me or actually *wanting* to be married to me or anything silly like that. I figured that as long as we're honest and totally up-front with each other, everything should work out all right."

"I see," he said, suddenly feeling his hamburger weighing heavily in his stomach. "We're treating this as a business deal," he repeated in a hollow voice. He took a long drink to relieve his suddenly very dry throat.

"Exactly. Of course we don't need to tell anybody else the truth. We'll just let all the family and friends think we're madly in love with each other." She chuckled. "That will be a shock to lots of 'em, I'm sure...Travis Kane finally falling for somebody and wanting to settle down after all this time. I guess the joke will be on them."

Travis felt as though he'd just seen the door slam shut on a trap of his own making. How could he ever admit to Megan now that he did love her without her immediately doubting him and his motives? The irony of the situation didn't escape him. She could accept that he might be willing to help her as a friend, but obviously would never believe he might be in love with her.

Wow! He'd really done it this time, hadn't he? He'd set up a situation where he was going to be walking a very thin line pretending they were no more than buddies and pals. After all this time, he'd managed to get stuck with an undeserved reputation for being a heartbreaker. In the end, *he* could very well be the one with a broken heart.

If so, he'd only have himself to blame...for not telling her the truth about his feelings years ago. His lack of courage back then could cost him plenty. His only hope was that somehow, someway, she would end up falling in love with him, too.

Five

Travis pulled into one of the shopping malls near the highway they'd followed into Austin. They hadn't talked much after their stop for food. He'd asked a few questions about the ranch, and she had answered easily enough. He guessed she'd come to terms with her reasons for marrying him and was now dealing with the consequences of her decision.

He hadn't realized just how difficult being with her and covering his true feelings was going to be.

Travis reached for her hand and they crossed the huge parking lot and entered the air-conditioned mall, taking their time looking at all the window displays and watching the other shoppers.

He discovered, to his surprise, that he was enjoying just being with her. She'd never pulled her hand away from his and he reveled in the slight contact. He could scarcely hide his need to laugh out loud at this enactment of all his adolescent dreams.

Megan O'Brien had agreed to marry him. Why, it was all he could do not to throw his hat in the air and let out a big yahoo! of a yell.

Eventually in their wanderings, they came upon a jewelry store. Travis paused in front of it, then looked down at her. "Well . . . we found what we were lookin' for, right?" She seemed to hesitate so he gave her hand a little tug and they walked inside the store.

"Good afternoon," the smiling clerk said by way of greeting. "How may I help you?"

With all the aplomb he could muster, Travis said, "We want to look at matching wedding rings," he said.

"Certainly, sir. They're over at the far counter. I'll be right with you."

Travis led the way to the back of the store to where the clerk had pointed.

"Do you mean you intend to wear a ring, as well?" she asked.

He eyed her a little cautiously, trying to figure out her mood. "You have a problem with that?" he finally asked.

"Oh! Of course not. I guess I'm just surprised. I thought the ring was going to be for show, to make all of this more convincing."

He nodded. "The engagement ring will be. It leaves no doubt about our intentions." He glanced down at the sets of rings on display. "Do you see anything you like?"

She laughed nervously. "I don't know anything about rings, Travis. I've never owned one."

"Not even a high school ring?"

She shook her head. "I figured it was a waste of money we could better use elsewhere."

He shook his head, feeling his dismay wash over him. "I wish I'd realized what you and the girls were going through back then. I guess I was too young to fully understand."

"Why should you? None of it had anything to do with you."

He stepped back from the counter so that he could see her face, since she was seemingly concentrating on the rings beneath the glass. He'd heard a peculiar tone in her voice, but could tell nothing from her expression.

"Now, then," the clerk said, arriving behind the counter. "What would you like to see?"

Travis studied the display for several minutes before he pointed out a set. The clerk placed the rings on top of the counter. "What do you think?" Travis asked Megan.

"Aren't they too expensive?" she whispered.

"No. Do you want to try one on?"

The clerk said, "You can have it sized to fit your finger, of course."

When she hesitated, Travis took the engagement ring and slid it on her finger. It fit as though it had been made for her. "I like it," he said in a matter-of-fact voice. "Do you?"

"It's beautiful," she said, her voice unsteady.

He nodded to the clerk. "Fine. We'll take the set."

The clerk measured his finger, then explained they would have to have his sized. "No problem." Travis took out his checkbook and wrote a check. "That's my address. Have it mailed to me. Meanwhile, we'll take hers with us."

When they walked out of the store, Travis looked at Megan and said, "You're sure quiet. Is something wrong?"

"I didn't know how quickly we could do that." She glanced down at her ring. "It's truly beautiful." When she looked up at him, her eyes were shining. "Thank you, Travis."

He took her hand and guided her into an alcove off the mall. Placing his hands around her face, he leaned down and kissed her softly. "You're quite welcome," he murmured when he finally raised his head.

She was staring up at him in surprise. "I—uh—"

"You might as well get used to me going around kissing you. It's all part of the window dressing. When we get back home, we're going to be convincing lots of people that this is something we've both wanted for a long time, but this was the first time I was able to offer you anything."

"People will wonder why you'd take on a whole family."

"Who cares what they think? Besides, I've got an older brother and a baby sister of my own. You'll be taking them on, as well."

She kept her gaze on their linked fingers and the sparkling ring on hers. "Not really. They won't be living with us like Mollie and Maribeth."

"Living with us," he repeated, grinning. "I like the sound of that. I think I'm going to enjoy living with you very much."

She jerked her head up to meet his gaze. "You know what I meant, Travis. We'll be sharing the same house and all."

"Is that what we'll be doing?" he teased, watching her blush.

"Of course."

He draped his arm around her shoulders and casually suggested, "Let's look around here some more then, after we get tired of window shopping, I know this great place to get some delicious barbecued ribs. After that, there's a band I want you to hear. I first heard 'em a few years back when I was in Dallas. I think they're really good, and I'd like to know your opinion."

He was greatly encouraged by the new light that seemed to be shining from her eyes. It was as bright as the sparkling ring she wore on her finger. His ring. His brand-new fiancée. Hot damn, but he felt good.

Travis gave her a quick hug before leading her back into the main part of the mall to continue their browsing. He no longer tried to hide his beaming grin.

It was past midnight when Travis turned into Megan's driveway. She'd dozed most of the way home, her head resting against his shoulder. With the change in speed and the turn, however, Megan lifted her head away and slowly straightened.

"I'm sorry. I didn't mean to fall asleep," she said, smothering a yawn.

"It's okay," he replied gruffly. "I know I've kept you out past your bedtime."

He parked next to the back gate. The yard light, positioned near the barn, gave off enough illumination for him to see her face. She looked pleasantly rumpled, sleepy and utterly adorable. His breath caught in his throat at the notion that this woman would soon be married to him and he wouldn't have to leave her and go to bed alone.

Travis turned in his seat and draped his arm over her shoulders, pulling her against him. "I guess I should let you go inside, huh?" he said, knowing his reluctance was obvious.

She drooped her head on his chest. "Um, I guess. I doubt I'll be able to walk tomorrow," she said with a chuckle. "My calf muscles are already complaining. I told you I wasn't used to dancing."

He slid his fingers through her hair and slowly massaged her scalp in a kneading, soothing motion. "You did fine, honey. Just fine. I was proud of you."

She tilted her head back slightly in order to see his face. Her eyes glowed in the light. "You were? I felt so awkward. And there were so many women there who knew all the steps and were watching you. It's obvious you're used to going out dancing."

He shrugged. "There's not much else to do after a rodeo lets out, unless you want to sit around the bars all night and drink. Since I'm not much of a drinker, I learned to do some of the line dances. They're kinda fun."

"Yes. Today's been such an eye-opener for me. I had no idea there were so many things to do and see. I can't remember when I've had such good tastin' ribs or so many! They just kept bringing 'em. It was surprising to find so many dance bands and clubs in the Austin area."

"I think it's time you started havin' some fun in your life, Miss Megan. You definitely deserve it." He picked up her left hand and brought it to his lips, placing a kiss on her knuckles, near the engagement ring.

She sighed and snuggled against his chest like a sleepy kitten. Did she have any idea what kind of effect she was having on him? His tight jeans were rapidly becoming tighter and more uncomfortable. He shifted and reached for the door handle.

"Thank you for showing me such a nice day," Megan murmured, slowly straightening so that her mouth was only a few inches from his. "You're really a very nice man, Travis Kane."

"No matter what anybody says, right?" he added with a grin. He was fighting his impulse to grab her and kiss her, reminding himself that his mama had raised him to be a gentleman, but it was a damn tough proposition to remember when the woman he loved was draped across him like this.

He quickly turned the handle and opened the door, then eased his leg down to rest on the ground. Instead of waiting until he walked around to the other door, Megan followed him out his side of the truck cab, so that he found himself wrapping his hands around her waist and swinging her off the running board to stand beside him.

She gave a breathless whisper of a chuckle before she slid her arms around his shoulders, went up on her tiptoes and kissed him.

He had to let go of her. He knew that. He knew that he needed to step back, fast, before she became aware of how strongly he was reacting to her, but the yearning he was feeling compelled him to deepen the kiss, instead, and he ended up pulling her even more snugly against his over-heated body.

Megan knew that she must be dreaming. This wanton woman in Travis's arms couldn't possibly be her! She was shy around men. Shy and awkward. How could she be so comfortable being pressed against his hard muscled body, content to allow him to tease her lips with his tongue, nudging them open so that he could explore the depths of her mouth.

His thrusts seemed to be causing his hips to sway slightly forward with every rhythmic movement of his tongue. She could feel the taut ridge of his jeans zipper rubbing sensuously against her stomach, creating the most unexpected tingling responses deep within her. She shifted restlessly, mimicking the movements he made with both his tongue and hips, her grip tightening around his neck.

"My God, Megan," he managed to pant after several heated moments. "We've got...to stop this...now...or else—"

He didn't say what else. Instead he gripped her arms and stepped back from her, his eyes blazing with heat and his features taut.

Already relaxed and half asleep when she climbed out of the truck, Megan wasn't certain her legs were going to be able to support her. Her knees gave way and she sank down to the running board of the truck.

Travis knelt beside her, his expression worried. "Are you all right?" he asked, his breathing a little more even.

"I'm not sure," she admitted, rubbing her hand across her face. "What's happening here, anyway? I feel so—so strange. I've never felt like this before. It's weird."

He touched her face lightly with his fingertips and traced the line of her brow, cheek and chin. "I'm sorry. I didn't mean to come on so strong."

"It isn't that," she replied. "I mean, you weren't doing anything I wasn't encouraging. I just didn't realize—" She shook her head. "Wow!" she said once again.

"I guess that's what happens when our hormones start kicking up," he said with a lopsided smile.

"Powerful stuff," she admitted.

"Yep."

After a couple of moments of silence she added, "Of course it doesn't really mean anything. It's like some kind of chemistry or something." She didn't want it to mean anything. She was afraid of what it could mean. The last thing she needed in her life was to fall for Travis Kane!

He didn't actually move, and his expression didn't really change, but he seemed to withdraw from her in some indefinable way. "It means that we're compatible, wouldn't you say?" he finally offered by way of explanation.

She leaned her head against the seat behind her and sighed, her eyelids drooping. "I suppose."

"It seems to me that a couple planning to get married would want that in their relationship," he said after a moment.

She forced her eyes open and focused on his. "Well, of course, if it was a real marriage."

Still kneeling, he clasped her hands between his much larger ones. "Believe me, Megan, this is going to be a real marriage."

She frowned, her mind still muddled with sleep. "But not a permanent one. That makes a big difference."

"I said that it doesn't have to be permanent. Your choice. I'm willing to make it as permanent as you like."

Something in his serious tone jump-started her heart, causing it to race. She swallowed. "You are?"

He held her gaze for a long moment before answering her. "Yeah."

"Why?" she asked, baldly, suddenly needing to understand what was happening between them.

"What kind of question is that?"

She shook her head in an effort to clear her fuzzy thoughts. "It doesn't make sense, Travis. I watched you tonight. There wasn't a female in the place who wasn't keeping an eye on you and wishing she was the one with you."

"You're crazy."

"No, I'm not. I know you weren't paying any attention to them, but I was. It was the same thing when we were in high school. All the girls wanted to date you. You must have run into the same thing during the years you've been on the road."

His frown had been steadily growing while she talked. "Is there some point you're trying to make here?"

"Yes! There is. I'm trying to understand what's going on here. Why me, Travis? Why, of all the women you know, are you willing to tie yourself down to me?"

He didn't answer her right away. He shifted his weight, still in a kneeling position in front of her. He cleared his throat and finally asked, "Are you going to believe me if I tell you that I love you?"

"Of course not!" she replied immediately with more than a hint of irritation. "That's ridiculous. I'm nobody special. I don't have anything to offer somebody like you."

He recaptured her hands. "Megan, don't sell yourself short. Listen to me, okay? Yeah, I've met a lot of women, women who saw me as some kind of trophy to win. Don't you understand? Once you're in any kind of limelight, there's always goin' to be people who are attracted to the idea of who you are, but they really don't see you, the person." He shifted once again, this time sitting alongside her. "But with you, it's different. You know me, the *real* me. The one you don't particularly care for that was always giving you such a bad time. But you see? We've known each other all our lives. Why wouldn't I want to be married to you? Look at it from my point of view. You're honest and dependable and extremely loyal. You're willing to accept being married to me without making any conditions."

She eyed him a little warily. "Such as?"

"Well, you know how important the rodeo circuit is to me, and how much I enjoy participating in the events, even though they're dangerous and I've been hurt a few times. You see, I've dated women in the past who insisted that I give it up because they worried too much about my getting hurt and because I traveled too much. But you're willing to accept me for who I am and for what I do without trying to change any of that. You can't possibly know how important that is to me."

She took a deep breath and held it for a moment before finally letting it go in a gusty sigh. "And if I decided after a year that I don't want to be married to you anymore?"

"The bargain would still stand," he replied promptly. "I'm not going to carry any unreal expectations about a future between us. I'll just take it each day as it comes and let whatever happens happen. At least I'll know I helped you out at a time when you needed it."

Her expression was earnest when she said, "You know I'll pay you back as soon as I have the money, don't you?"

"You don't have to do that, Megan. This isn't a loan. It was never meant to be. Remember that."

"I don't guess I'll ever really understand. It looks to me like I'm the one getting all the benefit out of this."

He turned so that he could kiss her very softly once again, without passion. Unfortunately for Megan her heart and body didn't notice the difference. Her heart began to race and her body seemed to turn into mush.

When he pulled away from her she couldn't look at him.

"I'm going to be leaving tomorrow," he said. "I'll be gone for three weeks. Do you think you can plan a wedding in that length of time?"

She shrugged. "What's to plan? Don't we just go to the courthouse, get the license and make an appointment with the pastor?"

"Yeah, and maybe invite a few friends and have a reception and—"

She nodded slowly. "I suppose that's going to be part of it, too."

"Our families wouldn't forgive us if we did it any other way. You know that. I'll be the first one in our family to be getting married. The same in yours."

"Maybe so," she reluctantly agreed. "It just seems to be a whole lot of trouble to go through for something that only takes a few minutes," she grumbled. She was sleepy and aroused and feeling a frustration she'd never before experienced.

Travis's deep laugh caused her body to quiver. "There aren't any other women like you, honey. You're definitely one of a kind.'' He tugged on her hand. ''Let's get you inside before you fall asleep sitting right here.''

Her leg muscles protested and she groaned. She reached down and took her shoes off. ''Remind me to never wear these kind of shoes again.''

''They aren't any higher than your boots.''

''It's the straps. My feet keep sliding around. At least the boots hug my foot.''

''Whatever you say, darlin'. But you looked really good today in your pretty dress and sandals—like a glowing sunbeam.''

She paused when she reached the back door and turned toward him. ''Thank you for a wonderful day.''

He took a step toward her, then stopped, jamming his fingers into his back pockets. ''I'll give you a call tomorrow before I leave…and I'll call you while I'm gone, so you can let me know what's happening around here.''

She nodded.

''I forgot to give you a check yesterday so I'll mail it to you on my way out of town. That way you can make the mortgage payment and not be worrying about it.''

''Oh, but you don't—''

''Oh, but I do. Let's not argue about the money. It's not that important.''

''Not important! Why, that's not so. That's the whole reason we're getting married, Travis Kane, and you know it. How can you—''

''Do you always have to go off like a short-fused firecracker? All I'm saying is that I want you to have it now and not have to wait until after we're married. Since the bank's being so hard-nosed about all this, let's not give 'em reason to refuse the payment, okay?''

Megan felt foolish, listening to his reasonable tone and rational explanation. She felt jumpy and on edge. She wanted him to leave and she wanted to throw herself around his neck and kiss the holy fire out of him. She couldn't remember a time when she'd felt so restless and confused.

She watched Travis take another step backward. He could hardly wait to leave, she could tell. "Good night, Travis. Take care." She opened the door and slipped inside the darkened kitchen.

She watched him through the window as he walked back to the truck. She didn't turn away until he swung the truck into a wide circle and headed back down the lane to the county road. Only then did she tiptoe barefoot upstairs and down the hallway to her bedroom.

Once inside her room she absently unzipped her dress and stepped out of it, dropping it on the floor. She walked over to the window and looked outside. Nothing was stirring. Even Butch's rooms there at one end of the barn were dark. Everybody was sleeping and now that Travis was gone, she was wide-awake.

She slipped off her strapless bra and half-slip, put on her shortie pajamas, then went down the hallway to the bathroom.

In a few short weeks Travis would be living here with them, having his meals with them, making a place for himself within their family circle. While she brushed her teeth she wondered what her mama and dad would think about her decision to marry in order to save the ranch.

Would they think she was wrong? Would they want her to sell it?

She rinsed her mouth, turned off the light and returned to her room. After getting into bed she lay there staring sightlessly at the room she'd had all her life. Everything about her life was changing. It was a scary feeling.

Just as the way she'd felt in Travis's arms tonight was scary. Something was happening to her. It felt as if her body was waking up to all kinds of things she hadn't known about. She wished she had somebody to talk to about all of this, but she didn't. She was the one the girls came to with their questions.

It was times such as now when Megan felt the most alone.

Six

"Hey, Megan!" Maribeth said, bounding into the room the next morning. "You planning to sleep all day? I need to know if it's all right with you if I go with Bobby and a bunch of the kids to Brady this afternoon. I forgot to ask yesterday before you left, and Bobby's already called to see— Megan? Hey, Megan, are you awake?"

Megan groaned and pulled her head out from under the pillow. "I am now," she grumbled. "I swear, Maribeth, you could wake the dead." She rolled over and glared at her little sister.

Maribeth wore her long hair in a single plait this morning. A smattering of freckles decorated her nose and cheeks. It was hard to believe that her baby sister was sixteen years old. She'd always been a tomboy, racing around with Bobby and his friends, determined not to be left out just because she was a girl.

Megan's eyes drifted closed. She knew she should have been training Maribeth more for household skills, but she'd left that up to Mollie. She didn't know much more than Maribeth about how to keep a house running smoothly.

Unfortunately she wasn't showing her much about how to keep a ranch running, either. Instead she had wanted her to enjoy her childhood and not be weighed down with too many responsibilities.

It was difficult to believe that Maribeth was the same age now as Megan had been when their parents had been killed. Megan couldn't ever remember being as young as Maribeth.

"Megan?"

Maribeth's voice sounded funny. Megan forced herself to open her eyes to see what was wrong. Maribeth had thrown herself onto the side of the bed. When Megan had turned over she'd let her arms fall across the bed in a sprawl. Now Maribeth was staring at her left hand, her eyes wide.

Oh, no. I forgot about the ring.

"What is it?" she asked, knowing full well what had drawn Maribeth's attention.

"I've never seen you wearing a ring before. Not ever. Even though we kept all of Mama's jewelry, I know Mama never had anything that looked like this." She touched the diamond setting as though she thought it might explode at any moment.

"You're right. It isn't Mama's."

"Then where did you get it? I never noticed it before."

"Travis Kane gave it to me yesterday."

Maribeth's eyes grew even larger, if that was possible. She stared at Megan as though she'd never seen her before. "Travis Kane gave *you* a ring? Why?"

"For the usual reasons, I guess." She hesitated, searching for the right way to tell her sister about the decision she'd made.

"Well, it looks way too expensive to be considered a friendship ring. The only other reason I can think of for him to give you such an expensive ring is because you're engaged to marry him," Maribeth said, obviously teasing her.

"That's right," Megan replied quietly.

Maribeth let out a shriek, then yelled, "Mollie! You've got to come quick and look at this!"

Megan scrambled to sit up. "For Pete's sake, Maribeth, calm down. There's no reason to carry on like—"

"What's wrong! What's the matter!" Mollie raced into the room, out of breath, then skidded to a halt beside the bed where the two sisters were lying. She stared at them as though looking for physical injury or some sign of impending annihilation. "Maribeth! What's wrong with you? How many times have I told you not to carry on like that? I thought somebody was trying to kill you!"

"The thought did occur to me," Megan muttered under her breath as she sat up and propped her pillow against the headboard and straightened the covers over her.

Maribeth ignored both of them. She was too caught up with her astounding discovery. "Megan and Travis Kane are getting married! Did you know that? Did she tell you? I can't believe she didn't say a word to anybody. She just—"

Mollie looked at Megan, her eyes filled with horror. "Megan? But I thought that we'd talked about—"

"Show her your ring," Maribeth demanded, bouncing on the bed. "Go ahead. Show her."

Megan slowly removed her hand from beneath the protective covers and reluctantly extended her arm toward Mollie. Mollie came around the bed and sat down on the

other side, watching Megan's hand as though it were a rat-
tlesnake.

"Megan?" she whispered, her voice shaking. In a
stronger voice, she asked, "Oh, Megan, I thought you'd at
least wait a while, give yourself some time to think it
through. I didn't think you'd actually— Oh, Megan, what
have you done?"

Megan reminded herself to stay calm. She'd already told
her sister her intentions. It wasn't her fault if she hadn't be-
lieved she'd actually go through with it. At least she had a
few weeks to talk to her, to convince her that she knew what
she was doing.

"I agreed to marry him, Mollie. It's going to be okay. I
promise. Everything is going to be all right."

Tears filled Mollie's eyes. "Oh, Megan."

"Come on, Mollie. You're supposed to be happy for me,
didn't you know? I'm actually getting married! Me, Megan
O'Brien...a bride!"

"Happy? That you've been hypnotized into believing
Travis Kane is serious about getting married, to you or anybody else?" Mollie said, her eyes flashing. She stared at the
ring but refused to touch her hand. "Did he give you the
ring to make you think that—" She paused, taking a deep
breath. "Did he try to seduce you last night? Did he? Please
tell me he didn't."

Megan scrambled out of bed and stared at her sister in
disgust. "Oh course he didn't seduce me, you idiot! Travis
isn't like that. He was a perfect gentleman."

Mollie shook her head. "He's just using you, Megan, for
his own mysterious purpose. Don't you see? He's softening
you up so you'll trust him and believe in him. Then he'll
walk away from you like he did all those other girls he used
to date."

Megan was getting angry. This was her life she was talking about, after all. And her decision. She could understand that Mollie felt protective of her and her feelings, but enough was enough.

"He told me he never wanted to marry those other girls."

Mollie just looked at her. "But he wants to marry you."

Megan nodded sharply. "Yes."

"Oh, Megan."

"You don't believe me?"

"Of course I believe you. It's him I don't believe . . . or trust."

"Well, you better get used to the idea because he's going to be your brother-in-law in a few weeks."

"Weeks! What are you talking about? Surely you're going to wait a while and see if you get along, see if he's going to treat you right. Did he promise to stop rodeoing?"

"Of course not. I would never ask him to."

"Is he going to stay here at all and help you run the ranch?"

"I'm sure he'll help all he can when he's here."

"I doubt that very much. Since he's paying good money to buy a—a wife and a ranch, he probably figures he's done all that's necessary."

"Mary Katherine O'Brien, how *dare* you say something like that to me! I am your sister and I deserve your respect. How could you think—"

Mollie threw herself into Megan's arms, sobbing. "I'm sorry, Megan, so sorry. I didn't mean it, I didn't mean it," she cried.

Megan began to cry as well. It wasn't long before tears streamed down Maribeth's face, too, as she patted first one sister, then the other. Eventually Megan blotted her eyes with a corner of the bed sheet, then did the same for Mollie and Maribeth.

"Would you look at us? Between the three of us we could end the drought we've been having! C'mon. That's enough sobbing and wailing. Butch has probably heard us and thinks we're holding a wake in here."

"Aren't you happy for her, Mollie?" Maribeth asked, looking wounded. "I thought you'd be glad that Megan has fallen in love with somebody. Why, she hasn't even dated anyone before." She looked at Megan. "Not even Travis! So why the sudden engagement?"

"Because it's what we both want," she managed to say. "He says he's ready to settle down and that he wants to marry me. He knows I won't try to change him and he knows better'n to try to change me. I think we'll get along just fine." She took her sisters' hands in each one of hers. "Please be all right with this. It's going to be hard for me to adjust to the idea, too. It's all happened so suddenly. But it's what I want. What he wants. Can't you both just accept that?"

"Of course we can!" Maribeth said heartily. She glanced at Mollie. "Can't we?" she asked hesitantly.

Mollie studied Megan for a long time before she spoke. "I just want you to be sure that you know what you're doing, Megan."

"I am sure."

Mollie patted her hand and stood. "In the long run, that's what counts." She scrubbed her face with her hand and forced herself to smile at them. "If I don't get back downstairs, the biscuits are going to burn. Come on down and get something to eat and tell us about your trip to Austin." She glanced at the ring, then quickly away. "It must have been quite a date."

Mollie hurried out of the room.

Megan turned to her baby sister. "Now, tell me again what it is you and Bobby plan to do today?"

"I'm really happy for you," Maribeth said. "I think Travis Kane is the handsomest thing. If I wasn't already planning to marry Bobby, he'd be the one I'd want to marry, myself."

Megan stiffened. "What did you say?" she asked faintly, feeling the shock of Maribeth's blithe statement hit her in the stomach. "You and Bobby are—"

"Oh, not for years yet, don't worry," she replied airily. "We've already planned it all out. We're going to college together—Texas A & M—and as soon as we graduate we'll come home and get married and live on his dad's ranch. His dad has already told Bobby that he'd build him a house on the place. After all, Bobby's an only child, so eventually the ranch will be his. In the meantime, he and his dad will run it and we'll get married and have lots and lots of children and—"

"Lots and lots—?" Now it was Megan's turn to question a sister's decision.

Maribeth laughed. "Oh, well. Maybe we don't have every single thing planned out yet, but we've still got plenty of time."

"I should say so. At least another six years."

Maribeth stood and stretched. "We aren't in any hurry. We've been best friends for years, ever since the first grade. I don't mind that you're getting married first. It makes sense, since you're the oldest."

Megan looked at her in disbelief. "I'm so glad you approve."

Accepting the comment at face value, Maribeth nodded. "So it's okay with you if Bobby picks me up to go over to Brady?"

"Since when is Bobby driving?"

"Oh, he's been driving for ages, but he finally got his driver's license a few weeks ago. He's a really safe driver."

Megan closed her eyes and sighed. She hated these judgment calls. She'd gone through it with Mollie and now it was Maribeth's turn. Of course, Mollie had never been one to run around with a bunch of friends. She'd been content to stay home most of the time and try out new recipes, and practice sewing, and baking and—

"Just be careful," she muttered, looking for some clothes to wear.

"Thanks, Megan," Maribeth said, giving her a hug. "I think it's great about you and Travis. He's going to be a terrific addition to the family." She darted out of the room and Megan listened to her noisy progress down the hallway and into her room. She shook her head.

In the morning sunlight she looked at her ring once again. If it wasn't for the tangible evidence, she could easily believe that she'd dreamed everything that had happened yesterday—shopping for rings, dinner and dancing. Was this what being married was going to do to her life?

She hugged herself before hurrying into the bathroom for a quick shower.

Much later that day, Megan was going over the accounts once again, this time making a list of what had to be paid, when Mollie poked her head into the office. "Can I interrupt you for a minute?"

Megan leaned back in her chair and stretched, smiling. "Please do. I need a break. I've been looking down my nose so long I'm getting cross-eyed."

Mollie came in and sat down across the desk from her. She was quiet for a moment before she finally said, "I owe you an apology for my behavior, not only for all those things I said this morning, but also for the way I acted toward Travis when he was here yesterday. I was rude to both of you. I guess I figured that if I told you not to consider his offer, that you'd see things my way. It was a shock to see you wearing his ring so soon." She shook her head. "It's really none of my business if this is what you want, and I had no right to say any of those things to you."

"Of course you did. You had every right to say whatever you want to me. You're my sister. We share whatever we're feeling about things, even if we don't happen to agree. We always have. You know that."

Mollie looked at her, her eyes damp. "The truth is, I guess I was afraid."

"Afraid? Of what?"

"Of losing you. You've been everything to me these past eight years—both mother and father—and I've gotten spoiled thinking that I would always have you in my life."

Megan leaned forward, resting her elbows on the desk. "You aren't going to lose me, Mollie. I'm not going anywhere."

Mollie shook her head. "I can't believe I could be so selfish. You've sacrificed the past eight years of your life for us, struggling to keep everything going, and now here you have a chance for happiness and I throw a tantrum." She reached over the desk. "Will you forgive me?"

"There's nothing to forgive. I understand. All of this is a shock for me, too. Believe me. I'm still wondering if I could have made it all up. I keep looking at the ring to make sure it's real."

"The thing is, I want you to be happy, Megan. You deserve it more than anyone I know."

"I'll be just fine. You'll see."

"Is Travis going to be able to help with any of those?" She nodded toward the stack of bills Megan had been sorting through.

"He's offered to, yes."

"I hope you aren't going to be too stiff-necked to accept his offer."

"I can't afford to be, Mollie. Like it or not, we need all the help we can get right now."

"Will he be coming over today?"

"No. He's leaving town today but he said he'd call before he left. He's heading back out on the road."

"Will you tell him how sorry I am for behaving the way I did?"

"Sure."

The silence that fell between them was a companionable one. Mollie finally broke the silence. "There's one more thing I wanted to say."

"Okay."

"About your wedding dress."

Megan smiled. "Oh, I'm not going to worry about that. I'm sure I can find something suitable that—"

"That's what I want to talk to you about. I remember Mama once said that she never had a wedding dress since she and Daddy eloped because he was going into the army. I was thinking that it might be fun if us three girls find a pattern we might all like and I could make a gown that each of us could wear when we get married. I would love to do that for you, if you'd let me. I promise to do my very best and if I get into any difficulty I'm sure Mrs. Schulz, my Home Ec teacher would help me with it."

"Oh, Mollie, what a marvelous idea!"

"You think so?"

"Oh, yes. We just can't let it give Maribeth any ideas."

"What do you mean?"

"She said this morning that she and Bobby are already planning their wedding for after they graduate from college. I just want to be sure she doesn't move the date up any because there's an available dress to wear."

Mollie's mouth twitched, and Megan snickered, then they both burst into laughter. When they finally calmed down, Mollie said, "Maribeth has been talking about marrying Bobby since she was eight years old. I really don't think we have to worry about their making any sudden plans."

"You know, I don't know where I've been all this time, but I didn't realize she felt that way about him."

"Oh, Megan, she's still such a child in so many ways."

"She's only two years younger than you are."

"I know, but I'm not all that sure she sees herself as anything other than one of the guys. She takes no interest in how she dresses or what she looks like. She's still as tomboyish as she ever was. A lot of her talk is habit more than anything. A carryover from childhood."

"Then you don't think I need to worry about her that much?"

"No, I don't. I rarely see them alone together anyway. Bobby's friend, Chris, is usually with them wherever they go."

"Now that you mention it, I think Maribeth did mention a group of kids was going to Brady with them today."

"That's what I mean. They're all buddies. I don't think that's going to change anytime soon."

The phone rang and Megan picked it up.

"H'lo?"

"Megan?"

"Oh. Hi, Travis."

Mollie slipped out of the room with a quick wave and shut the door behind her.

"How's your day going?"

"Fine."

"So how did your sisters take the news?"

"Maribeth was ecstatic. As for Mollie, well, she asked me to tell you how sorry she was for the way she behaved toward you yesterday. She admitted that she was a little jealous that her big sister was developing a life of her own."

"Oh!" His laugh sounded relieved. "Then it didn't have anything to do with me, did it? That's good to know."

Megan crossed her fingers. "Of course not. She would have reacted the same way toward anyone. At least she recognized what she was doing and why. In fact, she was just now mentioning that she would like to make me a wedding dress."

"Wow, that *is* a change of heart!"

"Yes. Yes, it is."

"Well, I'll leave here feeling a little better about things. Did you figure out how much money you need until I get back?"

She looked down at her list. "Yes, but you don't need to give it all to me now."

"Just tell me, okay, and I'll drop it at the post office on my way out of town. You'll have it by tomorrow. I'd bring it by your place today, but then I'd have a hard time leaving. I'm going to miss you, Megan. That probably sounds silly to you, under the circumstances."

"No. It doesn't sound silly at all," she replied, feeling shy. Somewhere between Travis's first kiss outside the jewelry store and the last one that had turned her bones to putty, she'd lost track of the purpose of this new business partnership.

She shook her head to clear it. "All right. Here's the total," she said, as though she'd been hunting for the figures. She read off the amount to him and said, "Is that going to be too much?"

"Not at all. So. When do you think we can get married?"

She chuckled. "You sound like an eager bridegroom."

"What's wrong with that?"

"Nothing, I suppose. I thought I'd go into town in the morning for the mail and stop by to speak to the pastor."

"I should be home by the fifth. Could we be married that Saturday? The eighth?"

"That's a lot of pressure to put on Mollie's skills as a seamstress."

"Well, why don't I give you a call in a few days, and in the meantime you can find out what she says, what the pastor says, and then we'll make more definite plans."

"Okay."

"Megan?"

"Mmm?"

"It's all going to work out just fine. Stop worrying."

"That's going to be a hard habit to break."

"That's understandable. Just try to remember that you aren't doing this all alone now. I'm going to be there for you. Maybe you can start off by letting me worry about things, okay?"

"Such as?"

"Where I'm going to sleep once we're married, maybe?"

"Travis!"

"Well, you never said."

"You'll have your choice. We have two empty bedrooms that we've been using for storage. One is the largest bedroom in the house, the one our folks used. None of us wanted to move out of our own rooms so we left it empty."

"Ah. A bedroom that's big enough for two. Now that sounds promising."

"Travis, please don't get any ideas about—"

"Too late. The ideas have already arrived."

"I'm not at all sure about that part of our relationship. I think it's just going to complicate an already complicated situation."

"Not if we don't let it."

"But we don't know each other well enough to—"

"Good Lord, woman, how many more years do we need to know each other before—"

"But we haven't gotten to know each other as adults, don't you understand? We haven't even seen each other in the past few years, or talked, or dated or..." Her voice trailed off.

"Or kissed? Or necked? Or petted?"

"You know what I mean."

"Okay," he said, chuckling. "Guess you win again. I promise not to badger you about sharing a room, or a bed. How's that?"

She was glad he wasn't there to see her face. She could feel it flaming. "Fine."

"I don't promise that I'm not going to be dreaming about you, though," he said in a husky voice. "I'm not responsible for what we do in my dreams. I'll be talking with you, Miss Megan. Bye now."

Seven

"Can't you stand still for just another moment?" Mollie muttered as she pinned the veiled cap to Megan's head.

"I'll just be glad to have all of this over. I can't believe the fuss everybody's been making."

Mollie stepped back and looked at her sister, standing there in one of the anterooms of the Aqua Verde church. "You look beautiful, Megan," she said softly. "Just beautiful."

Megan grabbed handfuls of the satin skirt and walked over to the full-length mirror Mollie had set up earlier. She stared at her image in surprise.

Once again Mollie had pulled off a miracle. The creamy satin gown hugged her breasts, ribs and waist, then flared over the hips into an ever larger swirl to the floor. The neckline dipped across her chest and hung just off her shoulders. The sleeves were long, ending in a point over the back of her hands.

The veil covered her face, but she could still see her face. She looked flushed, which wasn't surprising. She'd been rushing around all morning.

She turned back to Mollie who watched her with a smile. Mollie had not only made her wedding gown but with the help of friends had made her own maid-of-honor gown and Maribeth's bridesmaid dress. Mollie was in pale yellow; Maribeth in soft green.

Someone tapped on the door. Before either of them could answer Maribeth opened the door and slipped inside. She was holding a cluster of flowers. "Thank God your flowers arrived. Aren't they gorgeous?" Not waiting for a response she went on, "The church is almost full. I can't believe so many people turned out for the wedding."

Megan sighed. "I don't know why you're surprised. I think the whole county was invited."

"Well, the Kanes are telling everybody to come on out to their place for the barbecue reception. It's going to be great."

Travis's father, Frank, had offered to escort Megan down the aisle. Travis's brother, Zack, was his best man. The Kanes had been a godsend these past few months, helping with all the preparations.

She and Travis had been naive to think they could marry in three weeks. It was now the end of June, almost three months since he'd given her the ring. He'd been home only twice in that time, but during both visits he'd worked with her and Butch organizing needed repairs around the place.

He'd hired two more ranch hands to live on the place, which meant they'd had to build a bunkhouse near the barn to house them.

The extra help had been another blessing for both her and Butch. She'd overseen the repair of the windmill, and she and the girls had looked at paint samples to choose the color for the trim and the porch area of the house.

Everyone knew that Travis was paying for the improvements but nobody said anything. The townspeople and the surrounding ranch people appeared pleased that the O'Brien women finally had some needed assistance around the place.

Since everyone else seemed to accept the situation, Megan had worked hard to overcome her resistance to all the changes. Travis had assured her that he wouldn't try to run the ranch for her. He'd made it clear to the new hands that she was the one giving the orders, which appeased her somewhat.

However, when he showed up the second time with his arm in a sling and three cracked ribs, she'd suddenly come face-to-face with a brand-new fear—fear for Travis's safety.

However, he'd showed up at the church yesterday in time for the wedding rehearsal looking fit, taking the ribbing from all the participants, and wearing a cheerful grin. He was congratulated for having made it home in time to get married with no discernible injuries.

She hadn't seen him today. Mollie and Maribeth had smuggled her and her wedding clothes into the church before anyone else had arrived. All three of them had changed there.

There was another tap on the door. "Megan?"

It was Frank Kane, Travis's father.

Maribeth hurried to the door and opened it.

"It's time to get this show on the road," he said, looking around at each of them. "My, my, my. I can't remember the last time I saw such a dazzling bunch of ladies gathered in one small room. Y'all look smashing."

They could hear the organist playing in the chapel.

Mollie quickly knelt and rearranged the train to Megan's gown. When she straightened, she quickly wiped the corner of one eye. After a quick, silent hug, she went out the door, motioning to Maribeth.

Frank took Megan's hand and tucked it around his forearm. He patted her fingers. "I guess you know that you're making my boy a very happy man today."

She swallowed. "I hope so."

He smiled. "That young'un has carried a torch for you for years. I'd 'bout given up on him actually doing something about it."

His comments puzzled her for a moment until she remembered that Travis had told her he wanted everyone to think this was a love match. There was no telling what stories he'd made up to convince his family.

The music had paused moments before and now with a new melody, Maribeth was going down the aisle. As Frank had so aptly put it, it was time to get this show on the road. It couldn't be over soon enough for Megan. She'd never been cut out for all these fancy skirts and delicate veils. She'd take her jeans and boots over this stuff any day of the week.

She was halfway down the aisle when she saw Travis standing beside his brother. They both wore Western-cut suits—no sissy ruffles and tuxedos for them. As far as the men were concerned, women could get all dolled up to their heart's content, but wearing a suit instead of their jeans was as fancy as they intended to get.

In all the years she'd known him, Megan had never seen Travis wearing anything other than jeans. Now, in the black suit and the glossy black boots that showed beneath the flared boot-leg pants, he looked devastatingly handsome. His blinding white shirt emphasized his deep tan. He wore a Western bolo tie and his hair had been freshly trimmed.

For a moment Megan forgot to breathe. Here was the man she was about to marry, the man upon whom almost every female in the county had, at one time or another, had a crush. She'd been so busy planning for this day that she had lost sight of what today represented. In a few short minutes she would become the wife of Travis Kane...Megan O'Brien Kane. He would be her husband.

She lost the beat of her measured steps. Thank goodness they were close enough to the altar that it didn't really matter.

Megan turned her gaze toward Travis. He gave her his lopsided smile and a slow wink, then took her hand, rubbing his thumb over her knuckles.

The ceremonial words went by in a blur. Brief moments stood out clearly to her. Both Mollie and Zack produced the rings at the proper moments. Bemused, Megan stared at the glint of gold on Travis's bronzed hand. After a moment her eyes rose to search his. His face was solemn now, almost austere.

The next thing she knew Travis was lifting her veil and carefully draping it back over her head. "Hello, Mrs. Kane," he whispered before kissing her tenderly on her mouth. The pressure lasted only briefly before he raised his head. They turned to face the congregation. The pastor introduced them and the organ joyously released the refrains that accompanied them as they returned up the aisle together, Travis's arm wrapped securely around her waist.

Megan felt dizzy and disoriented by the time they paused on the steps of the church. Well-wishers poured out of the church behind them, quickly surrounding them, all laughing and talking.

"Are you okay?" Travis murmured.

"I don't think so," she whispered back, wondering if she was going to make a complete fool of herself by fainting for the very first time in her life.

To her astonishment Travis whisked her up into his arms, accompanied by more laughter and catcalls, and strode across the carefully manicured lawn to where his father's late-model sedan waited for them.

"Travis," she protested. "Put me down. I can at least walk to the—"

"Of course you can. Indulge me a little, okay? This is the first time I've had my arms around you in a while. Let me enjoy it while I can." His eyes were filled with amusement and his engaging grin tugged at her heart.

"What about the bouquet?" somebody yelled from the crowd who were following them across the lawn.

Megan glanced down at the flowers she still clutched in her hand. Without looking, she tossed it up and over her head amid cheers and whistles. She glanced around in time to see the look of shock on Mollie's face when the bouquet fell in her hands. Frank opened one of the rear doors and Travis placed Megan on the seat. He laughingly stuffed yards of satin in behind her, then closed the door.

Megan allowed her head to drop back and rest against the seat of the car while she listened to the buzz of conversation, laughter and jokes nearby. Someone was teasing Travis about his devastating effect on women. She could hear Maribeth's excited voice in the midst of the babble. Megan opened her eyes in time to see Maribeth push through to the side of the car.

"What happened? Are you all right?" she demanded, her eyes round.

Her little sister looked so grown-up in her dress. Bobby was standing a few feet away, excitedly talking to Travis...she caught enough words to recognize that rodeo was still his most avid topic of conversation. Mollie stood to the side, still holding the bouquet, her smile a little dazed.

How could so much change in such a short time? Megan had brushed away thoughts of the ceremony whenever it crossed her mind since April. It was just a necessary ritual to her. And yet... today she had felt the holiness, the commitment of what she was doing and she felt like the worst kind of sneak and liar.

Because he had wanted it that way, she had gone along with Travis's suggestion to let people think this was a culmination of a long-standing romance. People tended to believe what they wanted to, anyway. She'd never been the romantic type. She hadn't had time. Instead she'd put all her time and energy into hanging on to the ranch.

As a result of their marriage, the ranch was safe, which was what she had wanted, of course.

The door on the other side suddenly opened and Travis slid onto the seat beside her. Frank and Mona, Travis's mother, were getting into the front seat. They would now be driving out to the barbecue that was already cooking at the Kane ranch.

"Come on, Travis," somebody yelled. "You gotta kiss the blushing bride for us. We need to get a picture of this!" A camera was stuck in the open window.

Travis pulled her closer and laughingly kissed her with a loud smack.

"No, no! You gotta show some feeling here, man!"

"Not in front of the entire county, I don't," he retorted, making those who heard him laugh. "Let's get out of here," he muttered to his dad, who obliged him by pulling away from the curb with a honk and a wave. People started running for their cars, ready to follow them out to the ranch for the party-reception that had been planned.

Mona turned in the seat and said, "What a beautiful wedding, Megan. You and your sisters did a wonderful job of decorating the church . . . and your gowns are absolutely stunning.''

Megan felt her lips quivering. She was determined not to cry. Where had all these blasted emotions come from, anyway?

"I really didn't have that much to do with it. Mollie, Maribeth and several of their friends did all the work." She glanced down at her hands. "I'm not really good at that sort of thing."

"Your talent lies in other areas," Travis murmured, causing her to stiffen and stare at him in dismay. "You know as much if not more than I do about raising cattle, managing property, keeping up with the accounting—" He broke off with his list and grinned. "What did you think I meant, honey?"

"Now, Travis," his mother admonished. "Don't tease her. I swear you're the worst tease I've ever known."

"He is, isn't he?" Megan said, grateful for his mother's comment. "He used to delight in making my life miserable when we were kids."

Mona nodded. "Oh, I remember. Your mama used to call and tell me about the times you'd get off the bus in tears, vowing vengeance on that rascal." She shook her head. "I'd get on him about it, but it never did a lick o' good." She smiled at Megan. "I was sitting there during the wedding thinking about how proud your parents would have been of you if they could have witnessed what happened today."

"I like to think that they were there today," Megan replied softly. "If we never die—if our spirits live on—then I know that they were there today."

Travis squeezed her hand. He still had his other arm around her. "You scared me earlier. You were as white as a sheet. I thought you were going to faint."

"I was thinking the same thing. I don't know what came over me—maybe the crowd, the sudden heat after being in the air-conditioned church, or a mixture of it all."

"At least we don't have to worry about the possibility you might be pregnant."

"Travis!" Mona and Megan said in unison, their expressions of outrage almost identical.

He grinned unrepentantly. "Well? It's true, isn't it? Why are you shocked? Mom, I could see you being shocked if we'd announced that Megan *was* pregnant, but—"

"That's quite enough, Travis Franklin Kane," his mother admonished.

Travis and his father laughed. Mona turned so that she could see Megan and just shook her head. "I can't say I'm sorry to see him setting up his home somewhere else, but I must say, you have my sympathy, Megan, dear."

Thankfully, Megan didn't have to respond as they were pulling up at the Kane home where several people were already milling around setting up long trestle tables and tending to the meat being barbecued.

"I was going to change clothes but I forgot to get my bag at the church," she said, looking down at her dress. "I don't want to get it soiled, not after all the work Mollie went to making it."

"No problem," Frank said, stepping out of the car. "Travis can run you home. That's one nice thing about being neighbors."

Mona got out and waved at them while Travis slid under the wheel. "No use fighting all your slips and skirts for the short ride over there," he said, resting his arm on the back of the seat and glancing at her as he backed up and turned the car around. "I'll play your chauffeur, madame."

Just like that, they were alone. The car seemed to be filled with a silence that was almost tangible. Megan searched her mind for something to say, but her thoughts had scattered.

She was relieved when they pulled up in the deserted yard of the Circle B. Travis walked around the car and held the door open, offering her his hand.

Feeling ridiculously shy, Megan accepted his help and stepped out of the car. She picked up the front of her multilayered skirts and as naturally as though he was used to helping a bride, Travis took the train and draped it over his arm and followed her up the back steps.

The kitchen seemed to echo with emptiness. Together they walked up the steps and down the hallway to her room. She paused in the open doorway and looked up at him, feeling ill at ease.

"You're going to need some help with those buttons," he said quietly. "Mollie must have thought she'd be here to get you out of that dress."

Megan groaned. "Oh, I forgot all about them. I don't know why she didn't just put in a zipper."

He led her into the room and turned her back toward the window, where there was more light. "I can do it."

She fought to control her reaction to his touch as his fingers moved at an excruciatingly slow pace down her spine, from her neck to her lower back.

When he was finished he nonchalantly walked around to face her and without meeting her gaze, took the end of the sleeve of each arm, one at a time, and allowed her to pull her arms out. Holding the dress, he said, "Step out."

Most of the underskirt was sewn to the dress so that Megan now wore her strapless lace bra and a matching pair of bikini panties beneath a sheer half-slip.

She hastily took a step toward her bed to pick up her housecoat when he caught her hand. "Please don't," he said, his voice sounding husky.

She knew her cheeks were fiery red when she looked up at him. His gaze moved over her body, his expression wistful. "You are so beautiful, Megan."

Now that was a lie, and she knew it. "You don't have to say things like that to me, Travis. Remember? We're going to be honest with each other. I'm too skinny, my breasts are too small, my hips too narrow, my—"

"Hush," he said, pulling her into his arms and placing his finger across her lips. "You are a beautiful woman, inside and out. And you aren't too skinny. You're just right." His arms locked around her. "You're an exact perfect armful. What more could anyone possibly want?"

He replaced his hand with his lips, kissing her, nipping at her bottom lip, then soothing it with his tongue. He kissed and caressed her, his hands roaming restlessly up and down her spine.

She couldn't think when he kissed her that way. She knew that they needed to get back to the party. They were the guests of honor. They had wedding gifts to open and— Her mind began to reel, doing cartwheels in her head until she clung to Travis for balance.

His kiss intensified, his mouth hot, his tongue thrusting between her lips in a hypnotic rhythm. Megan felt a heated response from somewhere deep inside of her. She was having those restless sensations again that seemed to occur whenever he kissed her. She leaned into him and only then realized that sometime in the past few moments Travis had unfastened her bra. Now her bare breasts were pressed against his coat jacket. Feverishly she fumbled to unfasten the buttons on his shirt, loosened his bolo tie and with a soft sigh rubbed her breasts against his hair-roughened chest.

Travis continued to kiss and caress her mouth and face with his lips while he picked her up and placed her on the bed. He pushed the half-slip down, and stroked his hand along her hip and thigh, sliding over to her inner thigh then up until it rested on her curly mound.

Her eyes flew open and she let go of him, staring up at him in shock. "What are you doing?" she asked, her voice unsteady with the need for air. She realized that she was lying there with her slip around her ankles, wearing only her lacy thigh-high hose and her bikini panties.

Travis sank onto the bed beside her and ran his hand through his hair in disgust. "Losing my mind, that's obvious," he muttered, giving his head a hard shake.

She scrambled to sit up against the headboard and grabbed one of the pillows, hugging it tightly against her.

"I don't suppose it would do any good to say that I didn't mean for that to happen." He stood and walked away from her toward the windows. He kept his back to her.

She stared at the wide expanse of his shoulders beneath the coat. "I believe you," she finally admitted. "I didn't mean to unbutton your shirt and— Well, I don't know why I—"

He turned and looked at her, his shirt hanging open, pulled out of his pants. "We seem to catch on fire like a spark in dry tinder every time I touch you. I swear, all I wanted to do was help you with the dress. And then when I saw you standing there, I couldn't resist. I needed to touch you and taste you— I'm not trying to force you into anything. I want you to know that."

"Please, Travis. It's okay. Really. It's nobody's fault. It's like you said. Whenever we kiss we just kind of go—I don't know—crazy somehow. At least we know that's what happens. So we can avoid kissing from now—"

"Now, wait a minute! We don't have to go to that extreme, darlin'," he drawled. "I think I can control myself enough to be able to kiss and hold you without coming completely undone."

"Well, maybe *you* can," she replied with more than a little exasperation, "but I can't seem to keep my hands off you. It's so silly. I mean, I've known you forever and spent most of my life detesting you, and yet—and yet—"

"Yes?" he said, silently stalking back to the bed and leaning over her.

She pulled back closer to the headboard. "Travis, we don't have time to discuss this right now. We've got to get back to the party before everybody else gets there."

"The folks will tell them where we've gone."

"But still, it doesn't take all that long to change clothes. They'll wonder what's taking so much time!"

Travis straightened, his hands resting on his hips, and laughed without restraint. "Oh, honey," he finally managed to say, "they'll know exactly what's going on. We're newlyweds, have you forgotten?"

She slid off the bed, still holding her pillow as a shield and hurried to her dresser drawers. Opening one of them, she grabbed a pair of faded jeans and, with her back to Travis, dropped the pillow and hastily stepped into them, tugging them up to her waist. She filled them out quite nicely, Travis noted, still grinning.

Opening another drawer, she took out a plain white cotton bra and put it on, fastening it on the way to her closet. She pulled a Western-style shirt off a hanger, grabbed a pair of boots and walked over to the chair.

"Is that what you're wearing to the party?" he said, making no effort to hide his amusement.

She stood, stamping her feet into the boots and looked at him belligerently. "This is me, Travis. This is who I am. I don't own fancy clothes. I had to borrow the dress I wore the first time you took me out. If this—'' She looked down at what she was wearing. ''If *I'm* going to be an embarrassment to you—''

''No way, Megan. You could never be an embarrassment to me.''

He held out his hand. ''C'mon, sweetheart. Let's go enjoy our party. It isn't every day a person gets married. Let's make the most of it!''

Eight

Travis leaned against one of the stately live oak trees that surrounded the grounds of the home where he'd spent his life and watched his friends and family celebrate his wedding.

Somewhere in that throng was his bride, laughing at the jokes, blushing at the innuendoes, gamely going through the pantomime the day called for.

He'd really messed up earlier. He'd been moments away from taking her as if he were some undisciplined lout staking his claim, making her his wife in fact as well as name. He'd lost his head in the intimacy of the moment. That was no way to start out their relationship, not if he intended to convince her that they belonged together.

He was going to have to cool it, somehow, which was going to be much more difficult than he'd imagined during his long weeks away. Hadn't he planned how he would carefully woo and win her? Hadn't he thought all of it through, coaxing her to become used to his presence in her life?

At least now they would be sharing living quarters, another step in the process of establishing a permanent relationship with her. Didn't it help to know that she was as easily aroused as he was? He'd discovered today that she would be as passionate a lover as she was passionate in her zest for life. He had to make certain that he didn't scare her off by rushing her. One step at a time, remember that, he reminded himself.

"Travis? Why are you lurking here under the trees?"

He glanced around at the sound of his brother's voice. "Just thinking about things, I guess. It's probably not all that unusual, considering that today represents a traditional milestone in anybody's life."

Zack shook his head and grinned. "Better you than me, but then, you've had it bad for a long, long time. Megan hasn't a clue how you feel about her, does she?"

Travis smiled at his tone. "You noticed, huh?"

"Why haven't you told her?"

Trust his brother to get to the point.

"Because she wouldn't have married me."

Zack narrowed his eyes. "Care to run that past me one more time?"

Travis leaned his head against the tree. "Megan agreed to marry me in exchange for my help in running the ranch. She didn't want me to pretend any feelings for her and I realized if I told her the truth, she'd run in the opposite direction. So, I convinced her I could and would help her as a friend and neighbor and for no other reason. Lucky for me she had pretty much exhausted all her other options and she rather reluctantly accepted my offer." He threw his hands wide and said, "I'm her last resort. That's always good for a man's ego."

"Oh, I don't think we have to worry about the condition of your ego, bro. I'd say it's alive and well."

Travis shrugged. "I convinced her that we needed to pretend we were getting married for all the usual reasons."

Zack laughed. "Then I think Dad may have blown your cover. He told me earlier that he mentioned to her the fact that you'd been carrying a torch for her for years."

"When did he tell her that?"

"Just before he walked her down the aisle. He said she looked a little shocked for a moment. I can see why."

"Then she no doubt convinced herself that Dad didn't know the truth. She's determined to think of herself as incapable of attracting anyone. I decided to wait until the deed was done before I set out to convince her that my feelings are considerably more than friendly."

"How did you convince her to make such a commitment to you?"

"By telling her that she can end it in twelve months."

Zack shook his head. "Well, bro, I think you've been thrown off those bulls onto your head once too often. I'm afraid there's a real good chance you're going to end up with a busted heart as well as a busted skull if you aren't careful."

"To be honest, I fully expected for her to back out before the ceremony. That's one reason I hired the two guys to go to work over there. I gave her the money to pay the mortgage. I did everything I could to insure that she wouldn't renege on her end of the bargain."

"Why, you're like one of those dumb animals who not only knows it's headed for slaughter but actually races to get there. You amaze me, little brother, plumb amaze me."

Travis grinned. "Well, the way I look at it, I've got a year to convince her that I'm the greatest thing that ever happened to her and that she wouldn't be happy without me. I figure if I work it right the odds have to be in my favor."

Zack laughed and slapped him on the back. "Like I said, that ego of yours is alive and kicking, all right. C'mon, Dad sent me over here to tell you that it's time to get the music going for some dancing. And that means you've gotta lead that wife of yours out first."

Travis pushed away from the trunk of the tree and sauntered across the lawn to the swirling mass of people. "I can only try to make this marriage work, Zack. You know me. Stubborn as a mule. I'm determined to give it all I've got."

Megan felt a distinct tingling between her shoulder blades. She turned, wondering what had caused it. That's when she spotted Travis and Zack coming across the wide expanse of lawn toward the gathering that still lingered in the vicinity of the food.

Travis had removed his suit coat earlier in the afternoon, as well as his tie. He'd unbuttoned the top three buttons of his shirt and rolled up the sleeves above his elbows.

The trousers to the suit looked tailor-made for his lean, long-legged body, the slight flare below the knee to accommodate the boots adding to the graceful line of his muscular length.

She wondered where the two men had been. The only thing in that direction were the trees and the wooden fence of one of the horses' pens. Who knows? Maybe they'd slipped off to have a heart-to-heart talk. She smiled at the idea. She had a hunch there was very little that Travis hadn't already figured out about male-female relationships.

Travis walked up to her and hugged her. For the obvious benefit of the onlooking crowd he gave her another smacking kiss and said, "Hi there! Did you miss me?"

She grinned. "Desperately," she said, playing along with his mood.

"Now that's what I like to hear," he said, this time as though it was meant for her ears only. She gave him a puzzled glance. "Zack says it's time to begin the music . . . and we're expected to start off the dancing."

"Who made up all these rules, rituals and rites about getting married?" she replied with a sigh. "I've been getting all kinds of flack for my lack of proper bridelike apparel."

"Well, honey, you might notice that you're the only female here in boots and jeans and it's your wedding."

"Exactly. It seems to me that since it's my wedding I should be able to dress as I please."

He dropped his hands lower on her back, cupping her buttocks and pulling her up tight against him. "You haven't heard me complaining about those tight jeans, now, have you?"

"Travis!" She tried to push away from him in the midst of the general laughter, but his hold was too strong.

He nibbled on her ear and whispered, "Relax and enjoy it, honey. It's all part of the fun."

When she looked around, she saw the smiles and tender looks between some of the other married couples and realized that he was right. The joking and teasing was just as much a part of all of this as the flowers and the rings.

She relaxed and he immediately let go of her. "Let's go find some music." He took her hand and led her over to the portable tape player.

"I don't know how to dance."

"Of course you do. You danced with me in Austin."

"But that was different. They're going to expect something mushy and sentimental for the first one and I can't slow dance."

"Just follow me, baby. I won't let you down."

Thanks to Travis, it really was all right. He found a simple melody from a popular country-and-western album and led her to the concrete patio area near the house. After they completed a circuit around the area, the others immediately joined in. By the time the song was finished, the area was filled with dancers.

Another song began and Travis continued to hold her while others began to take part in some line dancing.

"That wasn't so bad, was it?" he asked, his voice pitched below the music.

"No. Thank you for helping me to deal with all of this."

"Hey, the worst is over. We've cut the cake, opened the presents. We can leave anytime now."

"Somebody asked where we were going for our honeymoon. That's the first time I'd even thought about one."

"I told the few who mentioned it to me that we planned to take one later, but that right now there was too much that needed to be done."

Mona walked up to them and said, "Where do you two intend to stay tonight?"

Megan looked at Travis, who seemed to be waiting for her to answer. "I, uh, thought we'd go home—I mean, to the ranch."

"Would you like for me to invite Mollie and Maribeth to stay here? I would imagine you'd like some privacy since—"

"Thanks, Mom, but that won't be necessary," Travis interjected smoothly. "The O'Brien house is plenty big enough for privacy, and we're all going to be living there so we might as well get used to it. However, I do think we're going to slip away from the party now. Megan's tired and I need to take the load of belongings that's piled in the back of my truck over there. Maybe you could have Dad bring the girls home whenever they're ready to leave, if they need a ride."

"Bobby Metcalf has his dad's truck. He can drop them off on his way home," Megan said.

Mona hugged them both and waved them off as they unobtrusively went around the house to where his truck was parked. At least nobody had tried to decorate it for him, which was a blessing.

"I figured you didn't want to hang around for a public send-off, considering everything," Travis said, helping her into the truck.

"No, please. I've really had enough of all this."

"You've been a good sport. But I really think it was necessary for the community to treat this as a normal marriage."

"Me, too." She impulsively leaned over and placed a kiss on his cheek. "Thanks for being so understanding."

Megan was pleasantly relaxed, which was surprising, considering that she and Travis were alone once again. She supposed it had to do with his nonchalant attitude, as though getting married and moving in together was just an ordinary occurrence, a logistics problem to be worked out.

They drove to her house once again and stopped near the back door. Travis looked over at her and said, "I want you to know that what happened here earlier won't happen again. I don't want you worrying about the possibility that I might pounce on you at any moment."

"I'm not."

Darned if he didn't look disappointed. She almost smiled at the thought he might be bothered by the idea that she trusted him. The fact was, she trusted him more than she did herself at the moment.

She couldn't forget how his kisses and his touch had triggered all kinds of new and wonderful sensations within her.

After all the rites and ceremonies today, she certainly felt married enough to at least consider the idea that there was nothing standing between their sharing the same bed and participating in all the intimacies of marriage.

However, she didn't trust all these new feelings. They certainly weren't reliable, not enough upon which to make such a decision. There was time...a year at least...in which to explore the possibilities of learning more about the pleasures to be enjoyed with her husband.

Megan climbed out of the truck and gathered up some of the bags Travis brought while he removed the boxed cartons and placed them on the porch.

With both of them unloading, it didn't take long to have everything in his room. The bedroom was a corner room and had originally been two rooms. An earlier O'Brien had knocked out the dividing wall and had partitioned part of the larger space to make a walk-in closet and a bathroom.

Megan went to the bathroom door and said, "You'll find towels and shampoo and soap in here. Sometimes I use this one when the other one's occupied."

"Why didn't one of you move in here after your parents died?"

"We talked about it. Several weeks after friends helped us to pack up all our parents' belongings, I considered moving in. The girls were so young at the time, they preferred their own rooms that Mama had decorated for them. The truth is, I felt the same way. Plus, I wanted to be closer to the girls in case they cried out at night. It's very quiet back here. You shouldn't be disturbed."

The bed was an oversize four-poster. She studiously ignored it. "There's plenty of drawer space for your things, and as you can see, the closet is huge. Do you want me to help you unpack?"

"Maybe tomorrow. I think we've done enough today."

"I'll see you in the morning, then."

"Megan?"

She stopped in the open doorway to the hall. "Yes?"

"You're still welcome to use this bathroom anytime. I don't mind sharing."

There was only one lamp on in the room, and his face was in shadows, so she couldn't see his expression. She nodded, not knowing what to say. The casual, friendly atmosphere had disappeared and she could feel the tension mounting between them. With a hasty "good night," Megan retreated to the safety of her own room.

Share the bathroom, share the bed. Share his life.

She couldn't do that. She couldn't allow herself to become vulnerable where Travis Kane was concerned. He had his own life, mostly on the road. She had her responsibilities here. What if she became too attached to him? She couldn't afford to miss him when he was gone, or look forward to his coming home. She certainly couldn't get caught up in worrying about his safety.

She just couldn't.

Early the next morning Megan was hunched over the kitchen table sipping her second cup of coffee when Travis came downstairs. Although it was light outside, the sun had yet to appear. She glanced up at him with a scowl before returning her glare to her coffee.

He grinned at the sight of her sitting there in her sleeveless shirt and coveralls, still barefoot, with her hair uncombed. "You find out all kinds of interesting things about a person you wouldn't have guessed unless you happen to live with them."

Obviously reluctant, she raised her eyes until her gaze met his. "What's that supposed to mean?"

He poured himself a cup of coffee, snagged the leg of his chair with the toe of his boot and turned it to face her before sitting down next to her. "That you get up earlier than I do, and that you're grumpy in the mornings."

She shoved her hand through her hair and reached for her cup. "You're reading a great deal into very little evidence."

He took a sip of the coffee and smiled. She made a mean cup of coffee. He could forgive a great deal in exchange for that particular talent. "True," he acknowledged. "Where did I go wrong?"

She folded her arms and rested them on the table. "I've been up for a while because I couldn't sleep." She shook her head in disgust. "I heard the girls come home, I heard every rustle in the yard, I heard—" She shrugged. "You get the picture. I've been sitting here trying to decide whether to try to get some work done or to go back to bed and hope to get some sleep."

"Ah. While I, on the other hand, slept very well," he said, stretching the truth more than a little. There was something about sleeping alone on his wedding night that created a certain restlessness, not to mention being aware of his new bride just down the hallway. However, he couldn't resist teasing his grumpy bride this morning. "The bed's quite comfortable, thank you for asking. I came down hoping to find you up and about. I have a suggestion to make. Why don't we spend today outdoors, maybe take the horses and have a picnic?" He took another sip of coffee, hoping to catch her reaction without being obvious.

Megan rubbed her head, wishing her nagging headache would go away. It wasn't fair that he could be so rested and relaxed, that he could sleep like a baby, while she tossed and turned all night.

"It will do you good to get away for a few hours," he coaxed. "Besides, I'm going to have to leave tomorrow. I'd like to spend a little time with you before I go."

She straightened. "You just got here."

"I know. But if I don't stay with my schedule I won't rack up enough points to qualify for world champion, which is what all this traveling is about. I have to enter as many events as I can." He leaned back in his chair. "I had to pass up a couple in order to come home for the weekend."

She gave him a disgruntled look. "I'm sorry if I put you out."

"Are you sure you aren't like this every morning?" he asked with mock suspicion. He had to tease her or he'd grab her and kiss the living daylights out of her. Damn, but she was adorable in this mood. No wonder he'd been unable to resist her when they were kids.

She buried her face in her hands and groaned. She peered at him through her fingers. "Oh, Lord, I don't know. I don't seem to know myself at all, anymore. I lay there last night wondering what I'd done. How could I have thought that marrying you would solve anything?"

Oops. He'd hoped that the ceremony yesterday had effectively moved them past this part of their relationship. "Well," he said, thinking hard, "at least your immediate concerns are taken care of. The mortgage is paid for another year, you've been able to take care of the most pressing repairs, and—" he threw his arms wide "—you got me in the bargain. Doesn't that count for something?"

The look she gave him was quite similar to the ones she used to give him on the school bus all those years ago. "That's what bothers me, if you want to know the truth. Our plans all sounded so cut-and-dried when we first discussed the idea. I mean, let's face it, I know you as well as I know anybody. I trust you. But now that we're actually married, none of it seems real to me.''

He let out a silent breath of relief. If she had to deal with these doubts, he was glad she was looking at them *after* the wedding and not before. At least now he had a better chance of dealing with them.

''Let's not worry about it just yet. I'm no expert by any means but it makes sense to me that marriage takes some getting used to. So why don't we just ease along, continuing with our routines while we spend whatever time we can together, and see what happens? Nothing has to be decided on today, does it?''

She'd been watching him closely during his speech, as though trying to make up her mind about something. He was glad he'd taken the time to shower and shave and put on his best pressed shirt. When she continued to study him in the silence that fell between them he lifted his brows in silent query.

After allowing the silence to stretch, she eventually asked, ''Are you always so bright-eyed at this time of the day?'' as though she really wanted to know.

''Only on alternate weekends,'' he immediately replied. ''The rest of the time I don't hear anybody or anything, much less talk, until the middle of the morning.''

He spotted a tiny grin lurking on her face as she said, ''That's good to know. I'd never realized before that unremitting cheerfulness too early in the day can be quite grating.''

''I'll keep that in mind.'' He got up and refilled both their cups. ''So, how about it, sunshine? You want to run for the hills today? After all, this is officially our honeymoon.''

She considered his earlier suggestion, not really finding anything wrong with it. She wouldn't have worked today anyway, which was one of her problems. She didn't know what to do with herself. Her life had changed when she hadn't been paying enough attention. She wasn't sure what to do next. "Do you have a particular place in mind?" she finally asked.

"Yeah, as a matter of fact, I do. I thought we'd take Daisy over to Dad's place by trailer, get my horse and ride back into a part of his property that he doesn't check out much. It would give me a chance to scout around and report to him how it looks, as well as give us a chance to do some exploring in a part of the county you haven't seen."

Megan stood and stretched. Either the coffee or the conversation had helped her mood. "I'd like that," she decided suddenly. She walked over to the refrigerator and opened the door. "The girls brought home enough food from the reception that we won't have to cook for at least a week. I could make up a picnic lunch."

He could feel his relief that she'd agreed to his plan run through his blood like the finest champagne. It was all he could do not to laugh out loud with triumph. Instead he nodded and said, "Great. While you do that, I'll make us some breakfast."

She looked around at him in surprise. "You can cook?"

"Yep."

"Wow. Maybe I got a better deal than I thought. I've often wondered what I'll do once Mollie leaves for college. I really don't function well in a kitchen."

He started gathering ingredients for pancakes. "You've got her convinced to go?"

"Yes. She got accepted at UT in Austin. I'm going to miss her but I'm glad she's going to get away and enjoy people her own age. She's had too much responsibility."

"That sounds funny, coming from you."

"Not really. That's why I understand the importance of a social life, so she won't be like me—awkward and unsure of herself."

He paused in his mixing. "Is that the way you view yourself? I see you as self-assured, filled with self-confidence, knowing what you want and striving to achieve it."

Why did his words remind her of some of the thoughts that had kept her awake most nights these past few weeks—thoughts of when she'd been in high school, wanting to be noticed by this particular man. Her feelings had been buried so deeply back then they were only now beginning to surface, which made her very self-conscious around him.

Megan began to fill a basket with food while Travis put their breakfast on the table. They worked together as though they'd been a team for years.

After they ate and were rinsing their breakfast dishes, Travis said, "Be sure to bring a swimsuit. There's a great place to swim in this particular section. Zack and I used to swim in this stream when we were kids. By the time we get there, we'll probably be glad to rest and cool off some."

A tingling awareness shot through her once again at the idea that she and Travis were going to spend the day alone together...and that he was leaving again tomorrow.

Hopefully she would get through today and have some time to work through this strange jumble of feelings before Travis came home the next time. She hated the jittery, jumpy feelings that had engulfed her recently. All she wanted was to return to the uneventful life she'd been leading before Travis Kane showed up and turned her life upside down.

Nine

By the time they reached the hidden canyon back in the hills, the sun was high overhead. They'd been riding for most of the morning through rough terrain. The unexpected adventure was just what Megan had needed to get her mind off her strange situation. Horseback riding had always been a way for her to relax and become a part of nature.

Did Travis know her that well to have suggested it, or did he find a similar sense of well-being away from the world? She was too content at the moment to ask him, but filed the thought away for another time.

Megan was surprised to discover that the Kane ranch, although sharing a border with the O'Brien ranch, had a different geological landscape on part of the land. There were more granite outcroppings, the hills were steeper, and she had seen a couple of natural springs that she wished they had on the Circle B.

Cottonwood trees and weeping willows lined both banks of the stream that ran through the canyon, providing shade for the horses and a cool place for a picnic.

The canyon was wide enough to capture the breeze flowing over the land. Since they had been steadily climbing, the air actually felt cooler here, despite the summer sun beating down around them.

"I don't know about you," Travis said, dismounting, "but I think I'm going to swim before we eat. I'd like to cool off some."

"Sounds good to me." She looked around the area and noticed that one of the weeping willows had an abundance of foliage drooping toward the water that could provide a private changing area.

She slid off Daisy and while Travis loosened the cinches on the horses she dug into the bag she'd brought for her swimsuit.

She'd had her suit for more years than she could remember. It was faded and without style, but it had never mattered to her before. Now, she felt a little self-conscious about being seen in it, but there was nothing to be done about it.

By the time she stepped through the leaves once again Megan discovered that Travis had already changed into ragged cutoffs and was already wading into the stream.

"How is it?" she asked, admiring the way his broad shoulders narrowed down into a trim waist. He was already brown from the sun, the muscles in his back gleaming.

He paused and glanced around. "Great, really great. I'm always amazed at how cold the water is, no matter how hot it is. The springs feeding this stream must come from way underground." His gaze took in her skimpy attire.

She self-consciously pulled her suit down over her hips, then hastily readjusted the top. She must have grown some since the purchase of this particular piece of apparel. Since it was all she had to wear, she couldn't be too choosy.

Luckily Travis didn't appear to notice what she was wearing. He had already turned away and dived beneath the water.

She sank into the refreshing depths with a chuckle. This was wonderful! There had been times when she was younger when she'd take the girls swimming in one of the stock tanks but this was so much better—cooler and fresher. She wished the girls were there to share it with her.

That's when she remembered that she and Travis were there together because they were married and people expected them to spend some time alone before he left again.

She was grateful that he'd come up with his plan to remove them from everyone. They hadn't even seen anyone when they'd brought Daisy over earlier in the day. It was almost as though they were the only two people in the world today.

Megan stretched out and floated on her back, closing her eyes. She wasn't prepared for the feel of something brushing her thigh. She let out a squeal as she jerked away and opened her eyes. Travis was standing beside her, grinning.

She'd gone under when she'd started trying to get away from what obviously was Travis touching her, and she came up sputtering. "You scared me to death!" she yelled, taking a swing at him.

He nimbly dodged her and hit the water with the side of his hand, splashing her full in the face.

"Travis!" She hit a spray of water back at him and in moments they were playing and splashing each other as if they were a couple of kids. He dived under the water and grabbed her ankles. She had a chance to grab some air so that as soon as she went under she twisted and hit him hard behind the knees so that he, too, collapsed.

Because of her smaller size, she was much more nimble and was able to give as good as she got. By the time they crawled out of the water they were both weak with a combination of laughter and strenuous exercise.

"I can't remember when I've acted so silly," she said, still giggling, as she grabbed a towel and scrubbed her face and hair. When she uncovered her head she saw that Travis was standing a few feet away, his hands on his hips, watching her with a grin on his face.

"What?" She asked, looking around. "Did you want this towel? What is it?"

He shook his head and without taking his eyes off her reached down and picked up his towel. "I was just enjoying watching you. I can't remember ever having seen you laugh before. I was just thinking about that. As I recall you were generally angry with me about something or the other."

She leaned over and began to dry her legs. "That's not surprising, since you always did your very best to make me angry!" She straightened and saw that he was absently patting his dripping chest, still watching her.

"Did you ever wonder why I pestered you so much?"

"I didn't have to wonder. I knew you hated me. Well, believe me, the feeling was mutual!"

His grin shone white in his darkly tanned face. He shook his head. "Wrong. Guess again."

She tied her towel around her waist and began to unload the food she'd stuck in the saddlebags. Travis spread out the blanket he'd tied to the back of his saddle and knelt down beside her, still watching her with amusement.

After setting everything out, she leaned back on her heels and looked at him. "What do you mean, guess again?"

"I didn't hate you. I've never hated you. So guess again."

She looked at him, puzzled by his attitude. "You just like to tease people?"

"Close. I always liked teasing you."

She snorted and began filling a plate with barbecued chicken, potato salad and spicy baked beans. "That's for sure," she said, taking a bite and giving a sensuous purr of pleasure.

He quickly mimicked her actions, and they spent the next several minutes indulging their appetites. At one point, Travis got a thermos of lemonade out of his saddlebag and filled the cuplike lid. They companionably shared the icy liquid between them while they ate.

"I'd forgotten how good all of this tastes," she said, licking the barbecue sauce off her fingers. "I guess I was more nervous yesterday than I thought. I didn't eat very much, and what I did eat, I don't remember actually tasting."

He stretched out on the blanket and folded his arms beneath his head. "You didn't act nervous."

She began to gather up their scraps and carefully stored the leftovers. She glanced at him from the corner of her eye. "I thought it was obvious to everybody, especially you."

"Nope. You acted like getting married was something you do all the time." He draped his hat over his nose with one hand while patting the blanket beside him. "Settle down and rest . . . let some of that food settle. Maybe we'll go swimming again before we leave."

She yawned. "My sleepless night is catching up with me now that I've filled my tummy." After placing the food back in her saddlebag she stretched out on the blanket on the opposite side from him. Within minutes, she was sound asleep.

Travis couldn't get enough of watching her. He could easily spend the coming weeks and months following her around, watching her many moods and listening as she dealt with life on the ranch.

She was so active, so vital, and most of the time so un-selfconscious. He found her fascinating. At the moment she was sprawled bonelessly beside him like a child. Her total innocence and lack of sexual awareness continued to keep him off-balance.

She seemed to take their skimpy attire in stride while he fought to control his response every time he looked at her. That was the biggest reason why he'd chosen to wear the cutoff jeans to swim in. They were more likely to camouflage his unfailing reaction to her whenever he was around her.

Travis had a plan, and he wanted to follow that plan, but he hadn't taken into account just how difficult being with her, living with her, was going to be for him when he couldn't make love to her.

He sighed, and closed his eyes. Even the thought stirred him. He was really in bad shape. It was probably a good thing he was leaving tomorrow.

He must have dozed off. The next thing he heard was a slight murmur from Megan. He glanced over and saw that sometime in the past hour or so, she had turned on her side and was now facing him. The strap to her swimsuit had slipped off her shoulder so that the top drooped across her chest.

Without giving the gesture much thought, Travis sleepily reached over and slipped his fingers beneath the strap to return it to its proper place. Her eyes fluttered open and she smiled at him, still more than half asleep, herself. His hand stilled on her sun-warmed arm. His fingers reflexively moved across the satiny skin.

"Did you sleep?" she asked.

"Some." He continued to stroke her shoulder and arm. Instead of replacing the strap, his movements slid it even lower, exposing a larger expanse of her breasts.

He kept his eyes on hers as he moved his hand until it slid inside her suit and cupped her. Instead of recoiling from him, she smiled and her eyes drifted closed once again. She arched her back so that her breast pressed deeper into his cupped hand. He bit back a groan.

This was insanity. She was still more than half asleep. He couldn't take advantage of her. And yet... and yet, he wanted—no *needed*—to touch her, needed a tantalizing taste of her sweetness.

Travis slipped the other strap from her shoulder and inched the top down her body until it rested at her waist. She smiled without opening her eyes.

He leaned down, touching the tip of her breast with his tongue, before sliding his lips around her, gently tugging.

She squirmed, her hips lifting slightly as she moved closer toward him.

He knew he didn't dare risk the strides he'd gained by getting her to marry him. However, he also knew he couldn't stop touching her. Not just yet.

He nuzzled her breast, first tugging, then soothing the pebbled tip with quick flicks of his tongue, moving from one to the other, placing soft kisses on the plump underside.

Languidly lifting her hand she touched his head, running her fingers through his hair. Her thumb caressed his ear. She continued moving her legs and hips restlessly.

Unable to resist such a seductive temptation, Travis continued to place tiny kisses in a meandering path across her breasts and down to her waist, eventually pushing her suit down... down... down her body and legs until it was removed.

He continued to caress her with his mouth and tongue, all the while cupping her breast . . . gently molding and tracing its shape with his hand.

He swirled his tongue in and around her belly button, causing her to moan and spasmodically move once again. When he raised his head to look at her, she was watching him, her eyes glittering.

"You are so beautiful," he whispered, his voice shaking.

"So are you," she replied softly.

He closed his eyes. "I've got to stop this. I can't—I know you—" He opened his eyes again.

"We *are* married," she offered timidly.

"Oh, yes. We're definitely married."

"Well, maybe it would be all right if— I mean . . ." Her voice trailed off.

He leaned on his elbow and looked at her with a burning intensity. "Will you let me love you?" he asked.

Her eyes seemed to grow larger as she stared back at him. He waited, not wanting to rush her. If she said no, he was determined to leave her alone . . . but he prayed that she wouldn't say no.

Slowly she nodded her head.

That's when it hit him. This wasn't why he'd brought her out here. He had thought— Dear God, what had he thought he was doing? She watched him, her face flushed, as though wondering what he would do next as she lay there beside him, wearing nothing more than a slightly apprehensive expression.

As though he was waiting for something—or someone— to stop him, Travis hesitantly placed his hand over her mound of tight curls, slowly slipping his fingers into her honeyed depths.

She was...oh...so warm there...warm...and slick with arousal. With an abrupt movement he reached down and unsnapped his cutoff jeans, then raised his hips enough to shove them down his legs.

Her eyes widened at the sight of his erection. He knelt between her legs, then braced his hands beside her shoulders and began to kiss her—long, possessive kisses...he tried to show her the familiar rhythm with his tongue, hoping she would understand and not be frightened.

When he lowered himself to her she gave a little whimper of impatience, sliding her arms around his waist and holding him tightly.

He rested against her briefly before he entered her, pushing slowly, easing a path. She was so hot and so tight.

She took control by the simple act of raising her hips to meet his careful thrust. Travis could no longer hold back and began to move in an overheated rhythm that quickly set both of them afire.

She clung to him, which further inflamed him, pushing him further and faster until he didn't have the strength to hold back a moment longer.

Megan let out a soft cry and tightened her grip around him and he gratefully recognized the spasmodic contractions that told him she had reached her peak. Her sudden cry had caused him to lose whatever control he'd clung to. His chest heaved in an effort to fill his lungs with much-needed oxygen, and he closed his eyes with a sense of joy and gratitude for what they had just shared.

Megan was his now. At long last and forever, Megan belonged to him. He would never let her leave him, not now. Whatever he had to do to keep her, he would do it.

"Are you okay?" he finally found the air to say.

"Mmm-hmm."

Her face was buried in the curve between his shoulder and neck. "I didn't hurt you, did I?"

"Uh-uh."

He wrapped his arms more snugly around her and rested his chin on the top of her head. "Are you ever going to speak to me again?"

She nodded.

"Then say something. Anything. What is it? What do you want?"

"More?" she asked dreamily, stroking his back from neck to buttocks before leaning back to look at him. Her smile had a definite smirk to it.

The relief he felt was overwhelming. "Oh, baby. You're something else," he whispered. "I was so afraid..."

"Afraid? Of what?"

"That you would hate me. We never really talked about this part of the relationship. I was afraid to bring it up. But when you said you didn't want to share your room, I took that to mean you didn't want to have an intimate relationship with me."

She sighed and allowed her head to drop back to his shoulder. "I didn't think I did. I mean—it's all so confusing. The marriage wasn't supposed to be real but somewhere along the way, during all the dress fittings, and plans and all, it began to feel that way to me. I guess I tried so hard to pretend that our marriage was just like everybody else's that I began to believe in it, myself."

He gave her a leisurely kiss. When he finally pulled a few inches away from her, he said, "I'm glad, because that's exactly what I wanted all along...a marriage like everybody else's."

She blinked. "You did?"

"Oh, yeah."

"Then why didn't you say something."

"I did. I asked you to marry me."

"But not because you loved me," she noted.

"Don't ever doubt my feelings for you, Megan O'Brien Kane. I love you, oh, my, yes I do. I have loved you since you wore pigtails down to your waist. Why do you think I gave you such a terrible time? I wanted you to notice me."

"Oh, I noticed you all right!"

"But you weren't supposed to hate me."

"Oh, Travis..." She kissed him. "This is all so confusing. My feelings are in such a jumble."

"It's okay, baby. You don't have to explain. If you'll just let me love you, and live with you when I'm home, that's all I ask. I don't intend to change any of the rules on you. Everything is just like it was."

She rubbed her hand across his chest. "Not exactly. I've never seen a naked man before. I'm not sure I'll ever forget that sight!"

He grinned. "Well, maybe being around a naked man on a regular basis will make it less strange for you." He sat up, grabbed her around the waist and carried her to the edge of the water. "Now I'll show you how much fun skinny-dipping can be!"

It was dark when they arrived back at her ranch. He told her to go inside while he put Daisy away. He watched her wander into the house and shook his head.

The older he got the more he realized that he didn't understand women. Not at all. He thought she would be upset with him for pushing the boundaries between them. At the very least, he had expected a stronger reaction when he told her how he felt about her. She'd appeared more bewildered than angry. He had to believe that her willingness to make love with him was a positive sign. She didn't appear to have any problem with consummating their marriage. One hurdle had been overcome.

He wished he hadn't already paid his entrance fees for this week's events. If he could spend more time with her, perhaps he could show her the kind of relationship he wanted them to have.

Then again, maybe they both needed some time apart, just to allow things to cool down. Nothing in their relationship had been normal from the very beginning. Why did he expect something different now?

By the time he walked into the house, Travis wasn't certain what was expected of him next. He felt more confused than ever.

Mollie and Maribeth were sitting in the kitchen.

"Hi, Travis," Maribeth said brightly. "It's weird having a man around the place. But it's kinda nice, too. Are you going to be here long?"

He removed his hat and hung it by the door. "As a matter of fact, I'm leaving in the morning." He forced himself to ask in a casual voice, "Uh, where's Megan?"

Mollie answered. "She's upstairs. She said she thought she rode too long today and she's sore and achy. I think she's taking a bath to ease her muscles."

Travis fought to keep his composure. Hell's bells, what had he done to her? Hadn't she been the one teasing him with—

"Well, uh, guess I'll head upstairs myself. I'll probably see y'all in the morning, then."

"Are you hungry?" Mollie asked behind him.

He paused. "No. We had a lot of food with us today. I'm fine."

"G'night, then."

"Night."

Travis went upstairs and down the hallway to his room. He didn't hear any noise from either the bathroom or Megan's bedroom. He would see her tomorrow, of course, before he left. He'd talk to her then, make sure she knew that he hadn't meant to hurt her or make her feel—however she was feeling at the moment.

He reached the door to his room and opened it. The bedside lamp was on, the covers were turned back and there was the sound of sloshing water in the bathroom. The door to the bathroom was open.

"Is that you, Travis?" Megan asked from inside the bathroom.

"Uh, yeah. I'm sorry. I forgot about your using this bathroom. I'll go back downstairs for a while. Don't rush on my account. I'll just—"

"Don't be silly. This is your room. Come on in."

He tentatively stuck his head around the corner. She had bubbles floating on the water of the old-fashioned tub. She had slid down into the tub so that her chin barely cleared the bubbles.

"There's room enough for you in here if you'd like," she offered.

Travis's heart did a double-time beat at the unexpected invitation. "You don't mind?"

"I wouldn't have invited you if I minded, now, would I?" She gave him a saucy grin. "Are you going to be shy with me?"

"No, of course not. I was just surprised, that's all."

"Well, c'mon in, then." She lifted a soapy arm and gestured to him.

Travis needed no further encouragement. He jerked his boots off, hopping on first one foot, then the other. He got out of his jeans and briefs, and crawled into the tub as he shed his shirt.

Megan was laughing even as the waves he made almost swamped her. She hastily sat up, pulling her knees up to her chest. She watched him settle himself at the other end of the tub, his long legs fitting around her.

"Aaah, this is wonderful," he said, feeling the heat soothe his body. He allowed his eyes to drift shut before he remembered his concerns. He straightened, opening his eyes.

"Are you okay?" he asked.

She smiled. "I'm fine. Why do you ask?"

"Maribeth said you were tired and that you thought you'd overdone the riding today."

Her smile widened to a mischievous grin. "I hardly thought it appropriate to explain to a sixteen-year-old what I'd been doing to create some unaccustomed tender spots on my body."

He leaned forward and slipped his arms around her, pulling her toward him and turning her so that her back rested against his chest. He hugged her to him, loving to feel her pressed so intimately against him. "I didn't mean to hurt you."

"You didn't. Not really. I was just a little uncomfortable for a while, and having to get back on Daisy didn't help matters. I'll be fine. I'll just stay on the ground for the next few days. There's enough work around here to keep me busy without needing transportation."

Their new position gave him access to her and he unashamedly took advantage. He cupped her breasts, leisurely moving his fingers over and around their plump roundness.

Her hands weren't idle, either. She caressed his thighs lazily, from knee to hip, trailing her fingers from side to side, lingering on the sensitive inner thigh area.

"I wish I weren't leaving tomorrow," he finally said wearily. "I never thought that—"

"That I'd fall into your arms quite so easily?"

"No! I didn't intend— Well, of course I'd hoped, but I wasn't going to take advantage—"

"Travis—" She turned her head so that her lips were almost touching his neck. "We haven't done anything wrong, you know. We don't know anything about the future, but for now, we can spend this time together, enjoy each other's company and see what happens."

"If I hadn't already paid my entrance fee, I'd cancel this trip, but this is an important event in the circuit and I—"

She placed her damp fingers across his lips. "I don't want to cause you to have to choose between me and what you do, understand? I wouldn't want to be placed in that position. I'm not going to do it with you."

He wrapped his arms around her waist and squeezed her gently. "We're going to make this work between us. I want our relationship to last."

"I'm glad. I feel like I've been dreaming this weekend. But if I am, I don't want to wake up. I had no idea having a husband could be so great."

He shifted, pulling his legs up and standing, hauling her to her feet at the same time. She turned and looked at him, puzzled.

Travis stepped out of the tub, lifted her out and briskly toweled her off. After giving his body a few quick swipes he took her hand and led her into the bedroom and over to the bed. He stretched out on the bed and patted the space next to him. She willingly slipped in beside him and he pulled the light covers over them.

Taking her into his arms, he said, "Do you remember my last year in school, when I was playing football?"

"Yes, of course."

"What I've never told you was that I was trying to work up enough nerve to ask you to go to the homecoming dance with me that year."

"Homecoming?"

"Yeah. Then two weeks before the dance..." His voice trailed off.

Her voice sounded strained. "My folks took us to Fort Worth for the weekend. The girls and I had gone to a movie matinee and they were supposed to pick us up after the show... only they never came back."

He held her close to him. "I just wanted you to know that even back then you were very important to me. I just didn't know what to do or say after everything happened. I remember you didn't come back to school for almost a month."

"I know."

"Even when you returned you were so distant. You attended classes, then disappeared back home."

"I was fighting to keep the girls with me. I was determined not to have them placed in foster homes. I was fortunate to be six and eight years older than they were. The added years gave me a bit of an advantage, but even so, it was really tough. I would have quit school if that had helped. Thank God Butch was there to talk to the authorities. He couldn't take legal custody, but he was there and several of Mama's friends insisted they were available to help supervise and offer advice if I needed help."

"I felt like I let you down during that time."

"How?"

"Because I wasn't there for you."

"I wouldn't have accepted your help."

"I know. I was afraid you wouldn't accept my offer this time, either. I knew you wouldn't believe me if I told you the truth about how I felt."

"You have to admit that I had good reason. I haven't seen you or talked to you in years."

"And you made it clear you weren't interested in me."

She curled up against him and brushed her lips against his. "I thought you hated me, that you lived to torment me. Besides, you always dated the most popular girls in school, the ones who could afford the fanciest clothes."

"Do you have any idea how sexy you looked—and still look—in your jeans and Western shirts? I got into a fight one time when one of the team members made a suggestive remark about you. After that everyone was very careful about what they said in front of me."

"I had no idea."

"Will you forgive me for hiding my feelings from you?"

"That depends on how you want to make it up to me," she said, her fingers wrapping around his rapidly hardening length.

With sudden motion, he rolled until she was beneath him. "I'll do whatever it takes to convince you that my heart was in the right place. I just wanted to be a part of your life."

She lifted her arms around his shoulders and pulled him down to her. "Well, cowboy, you finally got me into your bed. I guess you're going to have to show me some of those skills of yours."

Ten

A sudden gust of wind rattled the windowpanes and Megan glanced outside. The fierce autumn storm approached the ranch with dark roiling clouds rapidly covering the sky. Mother Nature seemed to be serious about reminding them summer was over.

She had spent the morning with Butch and the other two hands locating some of the stock and bringing them into pastures closer to the ranch building. Other than the wind, there had been no hint of a storm. Thank God they had brought the stock in from the outflung pastures.

Things were definitely looking up for the Circle B. The beef market was marginally better than it had been earlier in the year, and with any luck, the storm coming in would bring some much-needed moisture.

So much had changed in her life since her marriage with Travis. She wondered what she would have done without him. His generosity in advancing her the necessary money had made all the difference in the world to her. She was now able to meet her obligations, get needed repairs done and had the extra help so that she and Butch didn't have to put in such long, grueling hours.

Everybody had taken a break about one o'clock this afternoon and, since it was Saturday, the three men had gone off for the weekend, although Butch had offered to be home tonight so that she wouldn't be alone.

She insisted he enjoy his time off and spend the weekend relaxing with his friends. He had been working too hard for too long. She was pleased that he could rest more often now. He certainly deserved it.

Mollie was away at school, now. From her letters, she seemed to be settling in a little better now than the first few weeks she'd been gone when she struggled with homesickness.

Maribeth was involved with all the fall festivities in school. She was spending the weekend in town with friends.

The only thing that would have made Megan's day perfect was to have Travis home. She worked to keep those thoughts out of her head. He kept in touch by phone and gave her his itinerary so that she could keep up with his travel plans, but there were times, such as now, when she missed him so much that she ached with it.

Since their wedding, he'd been able to spend several weeks with her, but never more than two or three days in a row.

The last time he'd been home, he'd told her that what he hoped to do was to work with horses once he got too old for the dangerous competitions he presently entered.

He was already designing a new barn where he could board and service horses as well as break and train them.

Megan realized that part of her problem today was that she wasn't used to being alone. She wasn't sure what to do with herself. For years she'd kept a full schedule working on the ranch and looking after the girls. Now, they didn't need her all that much and the ranch was running more smoothly than it had in years.

She supposed it was time for her to discover what she could do if she didn't need to be working all the time. Not that housework or cooking appealed to her, but she might learn to enjoy having some time to read and nap.

She was curled up with a book in the living room sometime toward evening when she thought she heard—between the sudden gusts of wind—the sound of an engine coming down the lane. Maybe one of the neighbors had dropped by for a visit. That was a new event in her life as well, having time to sit and visit.

She hurried through the kitchen and opened the back door. The wind almost grabbed it out of her hand. She let out a whoop at the sight of her visitor, dashed across the porch and made a running leap down the steps.

Travis was home.

He'd backed the truck and horse trailer into the barn and by the time she got inside he had his horse in one of the stalls and was pouring feed into the bin.

"Hi!" she said, pausing in the doorway.

He glanced over his shoulder and grinned. "Howdy, stranger. I was wondering if this place was deserted. Where is everybody?"

He stepped back with the empty bucket, smoothed his hand across the horse's back and joined her in the opening of the stall. She stepped back so that he could latch the door. As soon as it was closed he turned and grabbed her up into his arms, swinging her around. "God, but it's good to be home! I drove most of the night to get here."

She was laughing breathlessly by the time he allowed her feet to touch the ground. "I wasn't expecting you for at least another week. What are you doing here?"

"I couldn't keep my mind on what I was supposed to be doing and I was making dumb mistakes. A guy could get killed not paying attention. So I decided to come on home. I just needed to see you again."

He swooped down and kissed her, a long, possessive kiss that made her blood sing. When he finally raised his head, he asked, "Where is everybody?"

"The men are gone for the weekend. Maribeth is in town."

"So it's just you and me?"

"Mmm-hmm."

With a whoop he grabbed her hand and headed toward the barn door at trot. "That's mighty obliging of everybody to give us some privacy, I must say. I'll have to—" He came to an abrupt halt and stared out at the ranch yard.

The yard was rapidly filling up with hail that bounced on the ground like thousands of marbles. The wind was so strong the tree limbs were bouncing and swaying. Megan paused just behind him, her head resting on his shoulder as she witnessed the end of the drought.

"Look, Travis," she said, pointing at what looked like a wall of water rapidly approaching them. "The rain is coming."

The greenish-black clouds continued to roll so low overhead she thought she could reach up and touch them. The wind carried the smell of wetness.

He wrapped his arm around her as they stood there watching. "We don't dare go out there now," he said, his voice barely heard over the howling wind. "If the hail doesn't get us, the lightning might."

The hail stopped as quickly as it had started. Within moments the rain hit hard, like a sudden waterfall. Megan took a deep breath, inhaling the scent of moisture that engulfed them.

Without a word Travis turned and, with his arm still around her, went back to the truck. He opened the door to the cab and reached behind the seat, pulling out a blanket. He dropped his arm from around her shoulders and took her hand, leading her to the ladder that gave access to the hayloft.

The expression on his face was all she needed to understand his intent. "Travis?" she asked, wondering at his audacity.

"Hey, this rain could set up its pouring for hours. We might as well get comfortable and get good seats to watch."

She started up the ladder and felt his hand brush across her bottom. Grinning, she stepped off the ladder and waded into the loose hay. The window at the end of the loft was open, but facing away from the force of the wind so that little moisture came inside. Sheets of rain swept past the barn.

Travis moved past her and paused a few feet away from the window, spreading the blanket. With his usual grace, he lowered himself to the blanket and lay on his side, holding out his hand to her.

"C'mere, you," he said, his voice sounding husky with need.

Feeling suddenly shy, Megan sat down on the edge of the blanket.

"Is something wrong?" he asked.

She shook her head. "I've missed you."

"Well, honey, I'm here now and you're wasting our precious time. C'mere." He took her hand and playfully tugged her down beside him.

"I forget what it's like being with you," she said, allowing him to unsnap the buttons on her shirt. "After a while, it's like I've dreamed it all...you and me...being married...everything."

"While I spend my nights dreaming of being home curled up in bed with you, holding you, loving you. I've lost my enthusiasm for the road since I married you." He slipped both hands beneath her shirt and slid it off her shoulders. While his hands were on her back, he deftly unfastened her bra and removed both items, leaving her bare from her waist up.

"You are so damn beautiful," he murmured, leaning over and kissing one of her breasts. "I dream of doing this to you." His warm breath gusted over her sensitive skin, creating a stream of chills across her.

Megan felt so strange. She'd been thinking about him, wishing for him, and now that he was here this all seemed too much like her fantasy to actually be happening. With a soft sigh of surrender, she discovered that she didn't care. If she was dreaming, she didn't want to wake up.

She feverishly fumbled to open his shirt and belt. He sat up and jerked off his boots, then reached over and helped her pull hers off as well. Their jeans soon followed.

The cool wind wafted over their nakedness. "What if somebody comes?" she whispered nervously.

"I'm countin' on it," he replied, grinning.

"I mean, company, or somebody?"

"In this weather? Not a chance. Even if they did, who would think to look for us up here?" He drew her back down to him and her thoughts scattered with the distraction of his chest pressed against her bare breasts. "Mmm," he said with obvious satisfaction. He ran his hand down her spine, cupping her buttocks, then pulled her up tight against his heavy arousal.

She shifted so that he was thrust between her thighs. With deep sensuous pleasure she undulated her hips just to feel his slick hardness move enticingly back and forth.

He bit back a groan and flipped her onto her back. Before her head stopped spinning he was inside of her with a hard driving rhythm that almost took her breath away.

She felt as though she was burning up for him, starved for the taste, scent and feel of him. She hung on to him with her arms and legs wrapped convulsively around him, fully expecting to go up into flames at any moment.

The tension climbed...higher...higher...until she cried out just as he threw back his head with a moan, each one triggering the other's release.

She sobbed with the beauty of the moment, wanting to capture and save this particular piece of time when she felt so much a part of him.

He rolled onto the blanket, never letting go of her, still panting for breath. She continued to place tiny kisses wherever her mouth could reach—along his jaw and his neck and his shoulder—even down to his chest where she nuzzled his flat nipple.

He continued to smooth his hands over her back and sides, following the smooth curve of her waist and hips, then lazily sliding to her front where he cupped and squeezed her breasts. Eventually he leaned over and pulled one of the rosy tips into his mouth, tugging lightly, while he caught the other one between his thumb and forefinger, gently massaging her delicate flesh.

She could feel him growing within her once again and she lifted her hips in invitation. A whoosh of breath accompanied his chuckle. "You're downright insatiable," he managed to say between his kisses and caresses.

"Me? What did I do? You're the one who—" She forgot her line of thought when he tugged on her breast with his mouth once again, then carefully stroked it with his tongue in a soothing movement. "Oh, Travis" was all she could think of to say.

It seemed to be enough.

The cold, damp air woke Megan and for a moment she was disoriented. Where was she? What time was it? Had she fallen asleep reading on the couch?

As she came more fully awake, Megan realized that Travis was curled around her, spoon fashion, so that only the front half of her body was exposed to the damp wind blowing through the open loft window.

The storm must have blown past them. The rain continued to come down in a steady, earth-quenching drizzle. The yard light that automatically came on at dusk cast its rays into the loft.

"Travis?" she whispered

"Mmm?" he replied without moving. He was still asleep.

"I think we can go inside now."

He tightened his hold around her waist. In his sleepy voice, he said, "I don't think I want to move."

"It's too cold to spend the night in the barn."

"I've got you to keep me warm."

She smiled into the darkness. "Not for long. I'm going in to take a hot shower."

"Spoilsport."

"You could always join me," she offered.

After a moment he stretched and straightened, rolling onto his back with a sigh. "Now there's an invitation and a temptation no man could resist." He began to gather their clothes, tossing hers to her. "C'mon. Nobody's here. Let's make a dash for it."

Giggling like children, they bundled their clothes and boots into their arms and made a mad dash across the soggy ground between the barn and the house wearing little more than when they were born. Once inside, they didn't slow down until they reached the bedroom upstairs.

With the help from the light of the hallway Megan felt her way into the bathroom and turned on the shower, tossing her clothes into the corner. Travis followed her into the small room. She glanced around at him and began to laugh.

"What's so funny?"

"You."

"Me? What did I do?"

"I just wish I had a picture of you standing there buck naked wearing your Stetson."

He grinned and readjusted it on his head. "Well, where else was I going to carry it? I had my hands full."

She walked over to him and with a new sense of assurance placed her hands around him. Her touch made him change rapidly in size. "Now, wait a minute. That isn't some kind of hat rack, woman."

"Of course not," she agreed. Stepping back, she motioned for him to follow her into the shower. He didn't need any more coaxing. He tossed his hat through the door into the bedroom and climbed inside.

The shower stall was roomy enough for two, giving her the space she needed to cover him in foamy soapsuds, from his chin down to his toes. She concentrated on the swirls and designs she could make on his chest, drew diagrams around his belly button and felt a particular sense of satisfaction when she heard him gasp when she meticulously soaped between his legs and around his hardened shaft.

She loved to watch the immediate responses to each of her soft touches. When he finally turned toward the water to rinse off, she wasn't certain which one of them was quivering the most.

"My turn," he said with grim determination, taking the soap away from her and making sudsy lather between his hands. Now she understood what he had gone through as she stood there trying to remember to breathe while he covered her breasts with soap bubbles. He lightly pressed...and gently squeezed...and intimately rubbed...until she was gasping.

"Why are you holding your breath?" he asked in an innocent voice.

She just shook her head because he was already exploring downward. His hands kept rubbing between her thighs, the heel of his hand pressing repeatedly on her mound of tight curls. She gave a quick sigh of relief when he knelt and continued washing and soaping her legs, ankles and arches.

Still kneeling he positioned her under the spray of water until the soap slid away from her body. Only then did he lean over and kiss her at that most intimate spot. She was already so aroused by all that he had done before that she could only moan.

He drew her out of the shower and quickly toweled both of them off, then carried her into the bedroom. Laying her sideways across the bed with her legs dangling, he knelt once again and with slow deliberation kissed and caressed her until she was sobbing with need. She was begging him for relief, for completion, for everything his lovemaking promised them when he finally stood and, wrapping her legs around his hips, joined them with a strong thrust of his body.

With his added freedom of movement he took control, varying his movements and his rhythm until she was once again whimpering. Slowly, stroke by stroke, he moved her into the center of the bed until he was able to stretch his length out on top of her, hastening his rhythm until they both felt the relief grab them, hurling them into completion and utter satiation.

Sometime during the night, Megan was roused by Travis turning them in the bed and tucking the covers around them both. As he hauled her back into the warmth of his body and contentedly curled around her once more, she heard him whisper, "You're going to be the death of me yet." She was much too relaxed to respond.

Eleven

The insistent ringing of the phone eventually drew Megan from a sound sleep. By the time she remembered that Travis wasn't there to answer it she was awake enough to realize it was in the middle of the night.

She fumbled for the phone, which was on his side of the bed. "H'lo?" she muttered, her tongue still asleep.

An agitated feminine voice replied. "May I please speak to Megan Kane?"

Megan blinked her eyes, trying to get them open enough to see the clock. The digital numbers said it was after midnight. "This is Megan. Who's this?"

"You don't know me. My name is Kitty and I'm a friend of Travis's. He's going to kill me for calling you but I thought you'd want to know."

Megan sat up in bed, clutching the phone to her ear. Travis had only been gone a few days. He'd stayed home longer this time than at any time since they had married.

He'd been reluctant to leave and she still hadn't gotten used to having him gone again. She leaned over and turned on the bedside lamp. "Know what? What's wrong? Has something happened?"

"Travis is in the hospital here in Pendleton."

"Oregon?"

"Yeah. You knew he was here for the rodeo?"

"Oh God! What happened?"

"He got throwed and gored and stepped on. The doctor has been working on him for several hours. Said he's lucky to be alive. He's got a concussion, some broken bones in his foot, as well as broken ribs and a deep slice along his side. But it's the concussion the doctor's worried about. He hasn't recovered consciousness since he was hurt."

"Oh my God. When did this happen?"

"This afternoon. Maybe nine hours ago. I figured you'd want to know."

"Oh my God," Megan repeated, her thoughts swirling so fast she was dizzy from the sensation.

"If there's anything I can do—"

"What did you say your name is?"

"Kitty Cantrell. I've known Travis since he started on the circuit way back when. He mentioned he got married a while back, so I thought— Well, if it was me sittin' there at home, I'd be wanting to know what had happened to him."

"Oh, yes, Kitty, thank you. You're absolutely right. I'll get there as soon as I can."

"Probably the quickest way would be to fly into Portland and rent a car, unless you want to charter a plane out of Portland to get over here to Pendleton."

"Thanks. I'll see what I can do. Can you give me the name of the hospital? The doctor's name? What room he's in?"

Kitty quickly gave her answers and she scribbled them down on the notepad beside the phone. By the time she hung up the phone, tears blinded her.

"Megan?" Maribeth stood in the doorway. "Who was that? Is something wrong with Mollie?"

Megan threw back the covers. "Not Mollie. Travis."

"Travis! What's wrong? What happened? Is he all right? Where is he?"

"In Oregon. I've got to fly out there. He's in the hospital, unconscious. They don't know for sure— The doctors think he'll be okay but they aren't sure because he hasn't regained consciousness." She rushed over and hugged Maribeth. "I've got to go to him."

"Of course you do."

"But I can't leave you here alone."

"That's not a problem. I'll stay with Kim in town. Her mom won't care. As soon as she hears what happened, she'll insist on it."

Megan tried to remember if she had a suitcase. She never went anywhere, but maybe there were some things in the storage room. She ran down the hall and opened the door to what they had designated the junk room. She found a dilapidated duffel bag in one of the corners and hurried back to her room.

Maribeth was already placing underwear and shirts out on the bed. "Gee, Megan, I hope he's all right. It would be awful if something happened to Travis. Y'all have only been together for such a short time. It doesn't seem fair."

Megan began to dress, not worrying about how she looked. She found jeans and a heavy shirt, then ran a brush through her hair.

"How are you going to get to the airport?"

"I'm going to have Butch drive me."

"Should I go wake him up?"

"Thank you, Maribeth, that would be great. I wasn't thinking that far ahead."

By the time she was dressed and packed, she heard voices in the kitchen and knew that Butch was already up and ready to take her to Austin. Thank God for Butch. He would be at the ranch to keep an eye on things while she was gone.

She hurried into the kitchen and saw him standing there, his hands in his pockets, waiting for her.

"Thank you for this," she said.

"It's the least I could do. You ready?" he asked, taking the bag from her.

"Yeah," she said, knowing that she was lying. How could she ever be ready for something like this? She'd never been out of the state, never flown in an airplane and now she was going to go racing halfway across the country to Travis's side. What had that woman—Kitty—said? That Travis wouldn't like it because Kitty had called her. Why? What didn't she know? Did that mean that Travis had been hurt other times and hadn't bothered to tell her?

She hopped up into the truck beside Butch and leaned back against the headrest as they began the two-hour trip to Austin. She would try to get booked on the first plane to the Pacific northwest. She could only hope that by the time she got there Travis would be awake and yelling at her for dashing up there.

He wasn't.

As soon as she reached the hospital, Megan explained to the nurses at the desk who she was. They told her that he had not regained consciousness. The doctors had done several sets of X rays to determine the extent of his head injury but she would need to discuss the results with them.

"May I see him?"

The nurse nodded. "The doctor will be making his evening rounds later today. He'll be able to discuss your husband's condition with you at that time."

Megan was glad she was alone when she stepped inside Travis's room. Late-afternoon sunlight flooded the room. The other bed in the room was empty. There seemed to be a cluster of machines surrounding Travis, all making their own peculiar sounds.

His skin looked pasty white except where there was massive bruising and for a horrifying moment she thought he was dead. Tears streamed down her cheeks, dripping off her chin despite her attempts to wipe them away. She tiptoed to the bed, uncomfortable with the sound of her boots on the tiled floor.

He had a cast on his foot, which was propped up. Massive bruises covered the side of his swollen face—mottled purple and green and yellow. One eye would probably not open even if he were awake to attempt to see out of it.

She sank onto the chair beside the bed and touched his hand. Megan had had several hours to think about what had happened to Travis during her flight between Texas and Oregon. She'd also had time to look at what had happened to her.

During the five months she'd been married, she'd become used to the idea of being Travis's wife. She'd accepted his long absences, had looked forward to his quick visits home, had reveled in their lovemaking, but until now she hadn't really allowed herself to admit the truth.

She had fallen in love with Travis Kane. It had happened so gradually that she wasn't certain when her attraction to him had become so much more.

Even though he had explained early on that he had loved her for years, she hadn't been comfortable with the idea that he was telling her the truth. She had no way to compare what he'd told her with what other men said when they tried to convince a woman they wanted them.

If they hadn't already been married at the time, she would have thought that Travis said that to every girl he dated, which was why they were so hurt when he walked away.

He hadn't walked away from her. He'd married her. Of course neither of their life-styles had changed much since the marriage. She still ran the ranch, he still traveled. But the routine had worked for them. She hadn't made any claims on his time, he hadn't tried to push her aside to take charge of the ranch.

Sometime during these past several months, Megan had forgotten the reasons behind their marriage and the fact that she hadn't intended to stay married to him when she originally agreed to the idea.

Now, as she sat beside him, she wondered how she could have been so blind to her own feelings. Was she so single-minded that her concerns were limited only to the ranch and her sisters? How could she have ever seen Travis as a means to an end rather than to love him and appreciate what he had done for her?

Yes, she loved him, but she had never told him. The grim thought that she might not be able to do so shook her tremendously.

Megan continued to sit there with him, willing Travis to open his eyes. She'd come a long way, not only in miles but in emotions, to tell him what was truly in her heart. She prayed that he would wake up soon and be able to hear her.

Hours later Megan stepped out of the room to get some coffee from the vending machine near the waiting room. She had spoken to the doctor who explained the procedures they had taken to check for injuries. He pointed out that the other injuries were healing satisfactorily and that hopefully

Travis would regain consciousness soon. Head injuries were always tricky and couldn't be predicted with any degree of accuracy.

Since there was no other patient assigned to the room for the night, the doctor gave Megan permission to stay with Travis. The large overstuffed chair would serve as a place to nap as she waited out the hours for him to regain consciousness.

She stopped at the vending machine and placed the necessary coins into the machine, then punched the button needed for the coffee.

"Excuse me. Are you Megan?"

Megan glanced around and saw a strikingly beautiful woman a few feet away, watching her intently. The woman's hair was so black it glistened. It hung long and straight, cascading across her shoulders and down to her waist. Equally black eyes, delicately tilted at the outer edges, studied her with an expression of curiosity and interest.

She wore a gold satin Western-cut blouse and black jeans that accentuated the long curving line of her legs. Her black boots gleamed.

"Yes, I'm Megan. May I help you?"

The other woman closed the gap between them and said in a low, husky voice, "I'm Kitty. I called you when Travis was hurt."

Megan's heart began to pound in her chest. This woman was Travis's friend? She was drop-dead gorgeous. Struggling to hide her reaction, Megan held out her hand. "I'm pleased to meet you, Kitty. I want to thank you for calling me."

Kitty took her hand. "How is he?"

"The doctor says he's healing nicely."

"Has he regained consciousness?"

"No."

Kitty's expression fell. "Oh. That's too bad."

Megan took her coffee and motioned to the empty waiting room. "Would you like to sit down?"

"Thanks." Kitty seemed to glide across the room as she led the way and sank into one of the chairs with all the poise of royalty. Megan felt awkward and unpolished, suddenly aware of her casual clothes she'd thrown on much earlier that day.

And yet—Kitty was also dressed in Western wear. On her the Western-cut blouse and jeans looked custom-made to fit her curvaceous body.

Once seated beside her, Megan gripped the paper cup with both hands. Staring at the black liquid, she fought to sound casual as she asked, "How long did you say you've known Travis?"

Kitty's smile flashed brilliantly white in her tanned face. "Oh, Travis and I go back a long ways."

That's what I was afraid of, Megan thought to herself.

"Are you part of the rodeo?"

"Yeah. I've been riding since I could walk. My dad was a rodeo bum, trailed around the country for years. He taught me to ride. I do some of the special events—trick riding and roping—that kind of thing. More exhibition than anything. I'm considered part of the entertainment."

Megan felt so out of place, not only because of the hospital environment but because she knew so little about Travis's life. She was certain that this woman knew her husband much better than she did, and she recognized that she didn't like the idea at all.

"I'm sure you've heard this a lot," she said, determined to be honest, "but I have to say that you are very beautiful."

Kitty smiled. "Thank you. I didn't have much to do with that. My folks are from Oklahoma—my mom's mostly

Cherokee and I look like her, although I got my height from my dad.''

"Travis's never mentioned you to me.''

Kitty glanced away before answering. "No reason why he should.'' She shifted her shoulders in a tiny shrug. "I always knew that there was someone waiting for him at home...and that's okay. He's always been there for me, a good friend when I needed one.''

Megan swallowed. Hadn't that been what he offered her as well...friendship plus the legal right to sleep together?

She shivered, wondering if she had misunderstood his intentions. Wasn't he the one who had said they didn't have to end the marriage after a year, that he was willing to consider their arrangement a permanent one?

However, now that she was being forced to look at the life he led when he wasn't in Texas, she was beginning to realize that there was a great deal about Travis she didn't know.

She didn't care what Kitty said about her relationship with Travis...the woman was in love with him. It was easy to spot when you suffered from the same ailment.

Kitty spoke. "Where are you staying?''

"Here.''

"No. I mean, what motel?''

"I didn't check into one.''

Kitty shook her head. "You can't stay here all night. You've got to get some rest, take a shower, that sort of thing.'' She reached into her handbag. "Here. I checked into the Best Rest Inn down the street once everyone else left to follow the circuit. I usually bunk with one of the gals who has a travel trailer. But I didn't want to leave town until I knew Travis was out of danger. Take my key and go get some sleep. I'll stay here with him until you come back. Okay?''

Once again Megan felt the odd throb in her heart at this further evidence that Kitty was deeply involved with Travis. However, she was exhausted, it was true. Not only the two-hour time difference, but the fact that she hadn't slept since the midnight phone call the night before all added up to a weariness she could no longer ignore.

Megan slowly reached for the key. "This is very kind of you, Kitty. I don't know what to say."

Kitty briefly flashed her beguiling smile once again. "No need to say anything. I don't want Travis to see those dark circles under your eyes when he finally decides to wake up. He'll think you've been in a fight with somebody." She stood and offered her hand to Megan, pulling her to her feet. "G'on, now. I'll stay with him in case he stirs. If he does, I promise to call you immediately."

Megan knew she was right. "Okay." She turned away and took a few steps. "I'll see you early, I promise."

"Don't worry about it. I'll be here whenever you show up. Sleep well."

Unfortunately, once she got to the room and into bed, after she fell asleep her dreams were filled with foreboding images and feelings that haunted her. She kept waking up with a jolt at every unfamiliar sound, and there were many. Even though the motel was set back from the highway, there were still sounds of heavy trucks passing through, as well as local traffic, blasts of car radio music and muffled voices.

She'd spent her life sleeping on a ranch where every sound could be immediately identified. City noises were as foreign to her as a jungle would have been.

Megan forced herself to go back to sleep each time, knowing she had to keep up her strength. Travis would need her and she wanted to be there for him.

When the phone rang she let out a quick shriek before recalling where she was. Light came through the curtained window and she realized that somehow she'd managed to sleep past dawn.

"H'lo?"

"Hi, it's Kitty. He's been stirring some. Hasn't opened his eyes or anything, but the doctor is encouraged to think he's coming out of his deep sleep. I thought you'd want to be here just in case."

Megan was already out of bed, standing by the phone. "Yes. I'll be there right away."

She dashed into the bathroom and turned on the shower. She'd been too tired the night before to do more than fall into bed. Ten minutes later Megan let herself out of the hotel room and hurried up the street to the hospital.

He was going to be all right! He had to be. She could hardly wait to see him again, to talk to him, to explain how she felt, to let him know how much she loved him.

She slowed her hurried footsteps as she neared his room and quietly pushed the door open. Kitty was standing beside the bed, holding Travis's hand. She glanced around at Megan, her face shining with relief.

Megan immediately looked at Travis and saw that his one good eye was open. He'd been gazing at Kitty, but when Megan stepped into the room, he glanced at the door and saw her.

He shut his eye for a brief moment, then opened it again, frowning. He looked at Kitty, his face registering his shock and disbelief, then back to Megan before saying hoarsely, "Megan? What are you doing here?" There was no sound of welcome.

Megan felt paralyzed as she stood in the doorway, feeling like an intruder. Travis had looked comfortably relaxed with Kitty before he saw her. Her presence certainly changed that. She forced herself to walk toward him. Kitty obligingly stepped back.

"Hello, Travis," she said quietly. "It's good to see you awake. How are you feeling?" She wanted badly to touch him, to reassure herself that he was all right. But the look on his face made her hesitate.

"What are you doing here?" he repeated.

"I was worried about you. I wanted to be certain you were okay."

"How'd you find out I'd been hurt?"

"I told her," Kitty said firmly. "I thought she should know."

Travis muttered something and closed his eyes. Whatever he'd said beneath his breath Megan knew wasn't particularly complimentary. When he looked at her again, he was still frowning. "I'm sorry Kitty called you. I'm okay. Just banged up a little. You shouldn't be here."

Megan felt as though he had slapped her. "I was worried—" she began but he cut her off.

"I'm fine. Really. This is nothing. You should get back home. If I need anything, Kitty's here."

Megan couldn't look at the other woman standing there so quietly. She kept her eyes wide, determined not to let him see the tears she was fighting.

"If that's what you want," she finally said around the lump in her throat. Afraid that she would betray her feelings at any moment, she spun around and walked out of the room.

After a long silence, Kitty finally said, "You can really be an ass, sometimes, you know that?"

Travis's head was hurting like hell and he didn't need anybody giving him a bad time. He felt as though every muscle in his body was screaming at him. His chest hurt with every breath he took.

"She wasn't supposed to know about any problems I have on the road. I've told you that. She doesn't know anything about the risks. I wanted to keep it that way, damn it!"

"Oh? And if you'd broken your fool neck, I suppose I wasn't supposed to let her know about that, either?"

He tried to shift in the bed and let out a groan before he could control it. "I'm not hurt that bad and you know it."

"No, as a matter of fact, I don't know it. What I know is that you're one stubborn, idiotic cuss of a man who's too afraid of losing his macho image to thank his wife for dropping everything to fly here to see about him."

"I don't want her worrying about me."

"Oh, that's a good one. Of course now she won't be worrying about you at all. She'll be too busy filing divorce papers to give you much of a thought."

He groaned. "You think I was too rough on her?"

"Try cruel. Whether you know it or not, you had all of us, doctors included, worried about you. You've been lying there unconscious for almost thirty-six hours. That's enough to shake anyone. It was stupid of me to think that a blow might have knocked some sense into your head, of course. I've watched you trying to kill yourself for the last several months, pushing all the limits with every event. I should be used to it by now."

"You know why, Kitty. I told you. I need all the prize money I can get. I'm trying to help Megan get her ranch financially back on its feet."

"Does she have any idea the kind of risks you're taking in order to make the money to help her?"

"Of course not. She doesn't need to know. Besides, I'm also saving to buy some horses. Once I've got enough money to invest into some good breeding stock I won't have to stay on the circuit like this."

"Well, if it makes you feel any better, you walked off—or should I say you were carried off—with the prize money here as well. Your scores beat out the other contenders. I picked up the check for you, which is why I've been hanging around, waiting to give it to you."

He touched her hand in a light pat. "You're a good friend, Kitty. You always have been."

She sighed. "Not good enough, it seems. I can't seem to stop you from ruining the relationship you've been talking about wanting so badly for years."

He tried to smile and winced. The entire side of his face was swollen and sore. "Maybe you should go find her for me so I can explain. I guess you're right. I didn't want her insisting on my quitting right now and I knew she would if she knew about some of my injuries."

Without another word Kitty hurried out of the room and down the hallway, looking for Megan. It was too late. Megan was gone.

After carefully checking the hospital corridors and lobby she returned to the room. "You're in worse trouble than we thought, Travis. She took you at your word. She's nowhere to be found."

Travis felt as though a herd of buffalo was trampling his skull. "Damn. I've got to talk to her and explain." He was having trouble concentrating. He closed his eyes, saying, "I'll give her time to cool down, then I'll call her. I've got ten days before the next rodeo. I'd planned to go home but maybe I'll wait until—"

"You're not doing anything with a cast on your foot."

He glanced down at his encased foot. "I've cut those damn things off before. As long as I don't put my full weight on it, I'll do all right."

"You're crazy, Travis. I've always known that. All you rodeo characters are."

"You should know, honey, you're one of us."

She shook her head. "Only because I don't know any other kind of life." She studied him for a long moment. "You want me to stay so I can drive your rig to Wyoming for you when you're ready to leave?"

"Where's your rig?"

"I had one of the guys drive it over to Boise for me. He's got a spread near there. I didn't know how long you'd be laid up, and I didn't want Blaze left unattended. Roy'll look after her until I can get there to pick her up."

"Thanks for the offer. I'll keep it in mind." He closed his eyes once again. "Give me some time to get over this granddaddy of all hangovers. Maybe, then, I'll be able to think better. Megan's going to be furious with me. She's got a temper that won't quit."

"You'll deserve anything she cares to dish out, cowboy. You need your butt kicked."

"Yeah, well, it won't be the first time I've been on her list of undesirables." His grin was halfhearted at best. "At least we're married now. Thank God. I'll make it up to her when I'm feeling better."

Twelve

"**W**hat in the hell do you think you're doing?"

Megan recognized the voice coming from below. She hadn't expected him to be home this soon. She wasn't prepared to see him. Not yet. Not now. Refusing to look down from her perch on top of the water tower, Megan concentrated on tightening the fitting of the replacement pipe she'd just installed to stop a leak.

"Megan O'Brien Kane! Get down from there before you break your fool neck."

Once the fitting was tightened enough to suit her, she threw her leg over the side of the supporting structure and began to lower herself down the ladder. She was not coming down because she'd been ordered to do so... she was coming down because she had completed what she'd set out to do.

Megan didn't take orders from anybody, most especially not from Travis Kane.

Travis's hands grabbed her around the waist before her feet reached the ground and he swung her around, causing her to clutch his shoulders for balance.

She hadn't seen him in weeks, not since she'd walked—correction, been *ordered*—out of his hospital room. She hadn't spoken to him since then, either. Not that he hadn't called, but she had always made certain that someone else answered the phone and told him she was unavailable. She'd had nothing to say to him.

She still didn't.

He looked thinner, which wasn't surprising. It was obvious that he hadn't been taking care of himself, which certainly wasn't her problem. He'd made that very clear.

"What are you trying to do, kill yourself?" he demanded.

She lifted her eyebrows as she met his gaze. "And if I am, what business is it of yours?" she asked, stepping back from him and walking over to Daisy.

"Why didn't you have one of the men do that?"

She paused without turning around, gathered the reins into one hand and stepped into the saddle before answering him. "I let them go."

Travis's jaw dropped at her calm announcement. "You did what? What are you talking about?"

She turned Daisy's head. "We can talk about it at the house," she said, leaning forward and signaling Daisy into an easy canter.

Travis lifted his hat and wearily resettled it on his head. Yep, he had really done it this time. He couldn't believe she'd stayed so angry this long for something he said when he was half out of his mind with pain and a blasted concussion. Hell, he didn't even remember what he'd said to her. The first few days after he'd regained consciousness had been a blur to him. Of course Kitty had been more than willing to repeat everything to him on more than one occasion when he'd been upset because Megan wouldn't take any of his calls.

All right. So he'd messed up. Hell, he was only human. Nobody was perfect, after all. Why couldn't she understand that she was the very last person he had expected to see when he woke up in that blasted hospital? Now she wouldn't give him a chance to explain.

No, wait. Hadn't she said she would discuss it at the house? He'd been so focused on finding her when he first arrived at the ranch that he'd done no more than make sure she wasn't around the house before getting directions from Butch as to possible whereabouts. He'd quickly unloaded his horse and come looking her... for all the good it had done him.

He looked up at the water tower. Damn fool woman had no business clambering around up there. Didn't have a lick of sense. And what had she meant by laying off the help he'd hired? She couldn't take care of things on her own. Hadn't she already learned that?

Travis made no effort to catch up with her. Instead he just followed the trail she'd taken. Man oh man, but he was tired. He'd driven long, lonely hours for several days in order to get back home.

God, he'd missed talking to her, seeing her. This was the longest he'd been gone since they were married. But his injury had set him back and he'd needed to make up for his hospital expenses and his missing some of the other rodeos he'd intended to enter before he'd gotten hurt. His ribs had been slow in knitting, his head had felt as if it was going to topple off his shoulders for weeks afterward and his ankle still bothered him.

Now he was through with the rodeo for the season. He had enough money to start adding to his stock. Who knew? He might decide not to follow the circuit next year. His ankle was still acting up on him. Besides, he was tired of all the traveling.

He missed Megan, he missed waking up with her curled up in his arms every morning, missed falling asleep with her beside him at night.

The problem was he had to get her to understand that he hadn't meant to hurt her feelings when she'd flown to Oregon to check on him. When he'd recovered from his injuries, he'd been touched that she'd cared enough to come... touched and encouraged. He just couldn't get her to take his phone calls so he could tell her so. He needed to explain if she would just get off her high horse and listen.

He rode into the ranch yard and nudged his horse into the barn. Spotting Daisy in her stall, he knew that Megan had already been there and gone on to the house. After unsaddling his mount and making sure he had his feed, Travis headed toward the house.

"Hi, Travis," Maribeth sang out cheerfully as he neared the porch. "How come you're limping?"

"My ankle's still a little sore," he said, negotiating the stairs with care. "Did Megan go inside?"

"Yep," she replied without moving from her position curled up on the porch swing. "She wasn't in the best of moods. Does she know you're home?"

"Uh-huh, which is probably the reason she isn't in the best of moods. I'm not her favorite person at the moment."

Maribeth grinned. "Yep, guess that's true enough. She acts like she never heard of you whenever I mention your name."

He shook his head with disgust and went inside. There was no one in the kitchen. He stuck his head back out the door. "Where's Doris?"

"Oh, Megan let her go. Said we didn't need a housekeeper. She insists she and I can keep up with everything."

"The cooking, too?"

Maribeth laughed. "Yeah. We eat a lot of frozen stuff these days, but I'm getting a little better at cooking. I really miss Mollie, though. She actually liked doing all that stuff. Can you imagine?"

Travis went upstairs to the room he and Megan had shared for the past six months. When he walked inside he immediately noticed that none of her belongings were on the dresser. He opened the closet door and found his things hanging alone. Not a good sign.

He went into the bathroom and stripped out of his clothes. If he was going to see Megan, he wanted to be refreshed as much as possible. He obviously had some serious fence-mending to do where she was concerned. He just wished he wasn't so tired. He felt as though he could sleep for a week.

By the time he returned downstairs, a meal of sorts was waiting on the table. Maribeth was filling the glasses with iced tea. There were two places set.

"Who isn't eating?" he asked, pulling out one of the chairs.

"Megan told me not to set her a place. She's working in the office this evening and took her dinner in there."

Travis knew it would be rude of him to join Megan and leave Maribeth to eat in the kitchen alone, particularly when he was fairly certain it was his arrival home that had sent Megan into the other room. He did his best to be polite and visit with Maribeth during the meal. As soon as they were finished, however, he excused himself as politely as possible and went to find Megan. It was time to deal with the situation, make his apologies and put all this behind them.

The office door was closed. Travis tapped lightly and waited.

"Come in."

He opened the door and spotted Megan working behind the desk. It didn't look as though she'd had more than a couple of bites of her meal.

"Megan, we need to talk," he began quietly.

She glanced up briefly, then tore a check out of the register. "Yes, we do." She watched him sit down across from her. "I managed to sell off most of my beef. Got a fairly decent price, I'm pleased to say." She handed him a check. "Here's the money I borrowed from you. I added the current interest percentage. I think that makes us even now."

He barely glanced at the check. "Megan, I owe you an apology and an explanation for the way I behaved in Oregon. I—"

"Not at all," she smoothly interposed. "You were right. I had no business going up there. What you do and who you do it with is none of my concern."

"Who I do it—? What are you talking about?"

"I've spoken to an attorney, explained our verbal agreement and that we are now ready to dissolve the partnership. He said—"

Travis came out of his chair in a lunge. "*What?* Now wait a minute! We aren't going to— I mean, you can't just— Megan? What are you doing?"

"Playing by your rules, Travis, just like always. I'm sorry if I misunderstood them for a while. You've been very kind, loaning me the money and all. Now that it's paid back I really think it would be better if you move out as soon as possible. I've already moved my things out of your room. I suppose you have to make some kind of explanation to your folks and will need a place to stay for a few days, but I really think the sooner you move, the more comfortable the situation will be for both of us."

He stared at her in disbelief. "Damn it, Megan, will you just listen to me for a minute?"

She folded her hands on the desk in front of her and looked at him. "All right... I'm listening."

"I was still groggy when you showed up at the hospital. I had no idea Kitty had called you. It was a shock—"

"Oh, I don't doubt that in the least."

"I realized only minutes after you left that I'd given you the wrong impression. Kitty went after you but she was too late. I didn't mean to sound so—so—"

"It doesn't matter. None of that matters now."

"It sure as hell does to me. You're kicking me out of here just like you got rid of the ranch hands and Doris. Hell, I've never been fired from being a husband before. You're not even giving me a chance to explain."

"Explain what, Travis? That your life is the rodeo? I know that. That Kitty understands your life much better than I ever will? I understand that, too. That on your few visits home you enjoyed playing house with me? Yeah, I finally figured that one out as well. I was very naive to believe that story you told about loving me all those years, but I don't guess I blame you for laying it on a little thick. The thing is, you didn't have to say all of that to me. You never forced me into doing anything I didn't want to do. I just didn't realize that you had someone on the road, that's all. You taught me a lot, Travis, and I—"

"You don't know a damn thing about what you're talking about. I don't have anybody on the road. There's nobody in my life but you!"

"Can you honestly look me in the eye and tell me you aren't involved with Kitty?"

"*Kitty?* Is that what this is all about? You think there's something between us? Well, you're dead wrong! Yeah, we've been friends for years. She's been like a sister to me. I've kept an eye out for her, let guys know that if they tried anything with her, they had to answer to me, but that's it. There's been nothing romantic between us."

"I see."

He eyed her uncertainly. "You believe me?"

She shrugged. "It doesn't really matter. I'm going to be able to make it now, thanks to your loan. I've ordered a herd of angora goats as well as several head of sheep to be delivered next week. I can't afford the extra help your money provided, which is why I let everyone go, but Butch is here. Between the two of us we can—"

"So you want to call the marriage off, is that it?" he asked in a low voice. "Just like that?"

"Yes, I believe that's the only thing to do."

"Why?"

"Because our life-styles just don't mix, Travis. I honestly thought when we talked about this, that you following the rodeo circuit wouldn't bother me, but that's before I saw you lying there unconscious, all battered and bruised, and I understood why you mentioned that others had tried to get you not to do such dangerous work. As long as I closed my mind and imagination to the danger, I was able to handle it, but no longer. It isn't fair to either one of us. You have your life-style and I have mine. They just don't have anything in common."

"What if I told you I was already thinking about quitting the rodeo? I've saved enough to start my horse farm, something I've always wanted. We could—"

"Not we, Travis. Not anymore. I think you should do whatever you want with your life. But don't include me."

"That's it? You want it over?"

She nodded.

He stared at her for a long time, taking in the shadows beneath her eyes, the tightness around her mouth. "I really blew it this time," he muttered.

"There should be no hurt feelings. That was our agreement, remember?"

"No, as a matter of fact, none of this was a part of our agreement. In the first place, I gave you that money. It wasn't a loan. In the second place, we agreed to stay together for twelve months... *remember?*" he used her same inflection on the last word. He stared at her but she refused to drop her gaze or respond to him. He spun away from the desk and began to pace, his mind racing furiously for some answers. "The way I see it," he said after a tense silence, "you still owe me six months as my wife."

After a long pause, she slowly nodded. "Technically I suppose you're right. But I thought since I've already paid you that—"

"Well, you're wrong. I don't want the money. I want those six months. I want to prove to you that we can make a go of our marriage, Megan. Will you give me that chance?"

She frowned. "I don't understand why you should care."

He gave a frustrated sigh. "Well, then I'll just have to figure out a way to make you understand during the next six months. I figure you owe this to me, Megan."

She drummed her fingers on the desk, fiddled with the fountain pen, straightened a stack of papers on her desk and finally sighed. "Do you really think this is necessary?"

"Yes. Yes, I do." He watched her intently, praying she wouldn't see his fear. He couldn't lose her. Somehow, he had to fight in every way he could to hold on to what they had.

The silence between them seemed to fill the room with its own tension-filled presence.

Finally she nodded. "All right. But I'm not going to sleep with you, or make love to you. I realize now that I should never have slept with you in the first place."

He folded his arms and looked at her. "Why not?"

"Because it muddied the water of our agreement. It complicated things. We should have kept it strictly as a business arrangement, without our feelings getting involved.''

"Are you saying your feelings are involved?" he asked softly.

"Don't worry. I can handle my feelings just fine. It was past time I grew up, anyway. You helped me do that as well. Guess I owe you another thanks for that." Her tone didn't sound particularly grateful.

Travis decided he'd gotten as many concessions out of her tonight as he dared push for. He turned toward the door. Just before he opened it, he paused and said, "I'll be home during those months. Since you got rid of the others, plan on using me. Just give me a list of each day's work schedule and I'll do my part."

She nodded without speaking and Travis walked out of the room.

He was so tired he could hardly walk straight and his damn ankle was throbbing like crazy. But he'd bought himself some time—not a hell of a lot, but it was better than having to move out in the next few days.

Somehow in the next six months he had to figure out a way to convince Megan that they could work all of this out together, if she'd just give them a chance.

He refused to think about the fact that he might lose her from his life. He couldn't lose her now. He just couldn't.

The winter schedule was slow. As more and more moisture fell, in the form of rain, sleet, and occasional snow, Megan found herself with time on her hands.

It certainly didn't help her peace of mind that Travis seemed to be permanently attached to the ranch now. He seldom left the place, giving a list to Butch of anything he needed whenever Butch went into town for supplies.

Maribeth seemed to be almost completely caught up with school activities. She'd gotten the habit of spending a couple of nights in town most every week, which meant that Megan and Travis spent the evenings alone at the house.

At first Megan had been nervous around him, waiting for him to argue with her, expecting him to use his charm to convince her to let him become a bigger part of her life.

He never said anything to her. Of course, there had been one time...

She sighed, thinking about Valentine's Day.

Now there was a day that she'd largely ignored most of her life. When her folks had been alive, her mother used to tease her dad about not being much of a romantic. One year he'd surprised her with a big heart-shaped box of candy. Her mom had been so touched by the gesture that she had saved the box, and used it for years to store special mementos.

In the years since her parents had died, there had never been any reason for Megan to give the day more than a passing thought.

But Travis had remembered.

Travis hadn't given her candy. He hadn't even mentioned the significance of the day to her. But when she went to bed that night she discovered a long-stemmed red rose and a sprig of baby's breath tied with a ribbon lying on her pillow. A square blue velvet box accompanied the rosebud.

She stared at the silent offering with uneasiness. What was he up to? Why was he doing this? Didn't he understand anything?

Reluctantly she approached the bed and picked up the rose, absently bringing it to her nose. Its gentle fragrance made her sigh. She'd never been given flowers before. Wasn't a red rose a symbol of love? Was that what he was saying to her?

Next, she picked up the box and lifted the spring-hinged lid. There, nestled on a bed of white satin was a golden locket on a chain. She stared at it, fighting back the tears that suddenly filled her eyes.

She wasn't a jewelry kind of person. She'd saved her mother's things for the other two girls who dressed up and went out. The only jewelry she owned was her wedding ring.

With trembling fingers Megan picked up the locket, only then noticing a small card that read, "I love you, Travis." She touched a small catch and the locket opened, revealing a carefully inserted snapshot taken on their wedding day. Travis had scooped her up into his arms—she remembered the scene so well—and had twirled her around as though publicly proclaiming her as his prize.

They'd both been laughing when someone—was it Mollie?—snapped the picture.

She'd put the locket and card away, unable to say anything to Travis about them, although she kept the rose until it turned brown.

Meanwhile, he quietly followed the routine she and Butch had, doing the work of both the men he'd hired earlier in the year, and making it look easy.

Being around him was having an alarming effect on her self-righteous anger. She was beginning to look at what happened from his point of view, which made it more difficult to hold him responsible for her hurt feelings.

The fact was that he *had* been concussed when he'd first seen her. He'd admitted to her that it was tough for him to have her see him in such a helpless condition.

What was particularly galling to Megan was her slow but inevitable realization that it was her jealousy of Kitty Cantrell that had convinced her that Travis couldn't possibly love her, Megan O'Brien, when someone like Kitty was an integral part of his life.

Eventually her sense of fairness made her stop and reconsider. Why didn't she believe that Travis could love her?

Well, of course it was simple. Just look at her.

She stood in front of the oval mirror in her bedroom one night, preparing for bed, and caught a glimpse of herself.

She looked more like a twelve-year-old kid than a grown woman. She could still remember Kitty's sultry good looks and voluptuous body. How could any man prefer her to Kitty?

But it was you he married, her mirror image pointed out. *Why do you suppose he did that? If he had wanted to marry Kitty, he's had plenty of opportunities to do so. And what if Kitty is in love with him? Does he have any control over her feelings?*

She was reminded of the girls who'd dated him in the past. It was true they had fallen for him, but he had done nothing to encourage them. Had he?

She shook her head at all the thoughts racing around inside. What was she going to—

"Megan? There aren't any towels in here! Can you bring me one?"

Oh, Lordy, she'd forgotten to replenish the supply of towels in Travis's bathroom. She was always forgetting some household chore or another. At least she'd remembered to gather up all the towels earlier today to wash them.

"Hold on!" she called back, hastily wrapping her bathrobe around her, "They're still downstairs. I'll bring you some."

She paused long enough to slip on her house shoes, then hurried downstairs and emptied the clothes dryer. Carrying the armful of towels she hurried back upstairs and down the hall to Travis's room.

She tapped on the door.

"C'mon in," he said, his voice muffled.

She fumbled the doorknob, managed to open it and walked into the room, dropping the pile of towels in one of the chairs. The bathroom door was ajar so she picked up one of the towels and stuck it through the door. "Here you go."

Before she could turn away, he opened the door, saying, "Thanks," as he began to dry himself off, seemingly oblivious to the fact that she still stood there.

Megan whirled away and headed for the bedroom door.

"Megan?"

She froze, unable to look around. "Yes?"

After a couple of beats, he said, "Thanks."

She quickly drew in some air. "No problem. Sorry I forgot to bring them upstairs."

He touched her shoulder and she glanced around at him. The towel was now wrapped around his waist and hips. "You don't have to act as though I'm going to attack you," he said quietly.

She turned to face him. "It isn't that, Travis. It's just—It's—" She waved her hand in frustration.

"What?"

She shook her head. "I don't know. This is all so confusing. I don't know what to do. I feel so—"

"So—?"

"Stupid! I mean, I don't know what's expected of me. I don't know anything about being married and in love and I know it's stupid to be jealous but I can't help it because I—"

He caught her by her upper arms and said, "Whoa, wait a minute here. What do you mean you don't know about—what was it you said—being in love? Would you like to help me understand that remark a little better?"

Megan couldn't possibly think with him standing so close to her that way. She was acutely conscious of the heat from his body, the fresh scent of soap he'd just used, and the unsteadiness of his breathing, as though he was just as affected by her. She looked up at his unusual, dark blue eyes and felt a melting sensation sweep over her. "You must know how I feel about you," she said weakly.

He caught his breath. "No. Maybe you'd better tell me."

She swallowed, then, unable to resist, she laid her palm lightly against his chest, feeling his heart race beneath her hand. Concentrating on the strong line of his jaw, she admitted, "I've loved you for a long time, Travis. I just didn't understand what I was feeling. I had a crush on you in high school, just like half the girls around. I tried to convince myself that what I was feeling was hate, but I—"

"Oh, Megan!" he groaned, gathering her up into his arms and holding her tightly against him. His towel immediately slithered to the floor. "Oh, baby, if you only knew how I've prayed that I'd hear you say that to me someday. I was beginning to give up hope."

He began to kiss her—long, drugging kisses that made her go limp. She felt the room tilting before she realized that he had picked her up and carried her to the bed. Her robe had fallen open, revealing that she wore nothing underneath.

Travis lowered her to the bed and quickly followed. He couldn't seem to decide where to touch and caress her next, both his mouth and hands moving restlessly over her.

"Don't you understand?" he whispered brokenly. "I never really saw another woman, not in school, and not on the road. You're the only one I've ever wanted."

"Oh, Travis."

There were no more words between them, not for several, love-filled hours. Sometime in the early morning, predawn, she lay awake, her head resting on his shoulder as he lazily stroked her breast. "Let's don't ever fight again, okay?" he whispered. "Not like that. If you want to yell and scream at me, okay, but don't push me away, babe. Anything but that."

Megan felt completely loved at that moment, as well as cherished and treasured. She smiled in the darkness. "I won't push you away," she admitted. "But I probably will yell and scream. You have a wonderful knack for provoking me to extreme reactions."

"What I can't understand is why you would ever be jealous of someone like Kitty?"

She could hear the sincere puzzlement in his voice.

"She's beautiful, Travis," she said pointedly, feeling much more gracious about the other woman's looks now.

"But she isn't you," he said in such a reasonable tone of voice that she found herself loving him even more than she did before.

"Travis?"

"Mmm?"

"Were you serious about not going out on the circuit this year?"

"Yes, ma'am, I'm definitely serious about that. I was having too much trouble keeping my mind on what I was doing those last few months."

"Can you use the money I gave you to start your horse farm?"

He was quiet for so long that she thought he wasn't going to answer her. She'd almost dozed off before he said, "We can decide that together, baby. From now on, we'll make all our decisions together."

Megan drifted into sleep.

Epilogue

"Uh, Travis, there's something I need to discuss with you," Megan said several weeks later.

It was April once more. The Texas winter had disappeared and the bluebonnets were in full bloom, their color still rivaled by the brightness of her husband's compelling eyes.

Travis was in the barn checking on the new foal. He'd bought the mare knowing she was due in the spring and was quite pleased with the results.

He stepped out of the stall and joined Megan who was leaning against one of the posts, watching him. He leaned down and gave her a quick kiss. "Sure. What's up?"

"It's almost lunchtime. Why don't we go eat now?"

"You're getting more domestic every day," he teased, dropping his arm around her shoulder and guiding her toward the door. "What are we having?"

She grinned. "Don't laugh at me. At least I'm trying. It's

one of Mollie's recipes she left with me during spring break. I'm actually discovering I'm having fun experimenting.''

They were halfway through lunch before Travis said, ''So, what is it you need to discuss with me? Is it your herd? Do you need more help? What?''

''The herd is fine, the extra hands are a godsend now that Butch is retiring, and yes, I think maybe we are going to need to hire a housekeeper.''

''Ah. So you aren't enjoying being domestic as much as I thought.''

''Well, it's not that, exactly. You remember when we agreed to discuss everything together before we made any decisions?''

''Uh-huh.''

''Well, I'm afraid we're going to both have to accept that we can't always be in that much control.''

''What are you talking about?''

''I'm pregnant.''

She hadn't meant to blurt it out that way. She'd wanted to break it to him slowly, gently. She'd wanted to be sure that he truly wanted to have a family and that he wanted to start one now. But all of that was a little behind times now.

''Pregnant?'' he repeated hoarsely before a smirky grin appeared on his face. ''No kidding? I mean, you're sure about that?''

She nodded. ''I bought one of those home kits to make sure, but I already knew. The signs have been too obvious.''

''When? I mean, when is it due?''

''November, I think. I've got to see a doctor to make sure but I think it will be here in November.''

Travis's grin grew wider. He reached for her hand and squeezed it. ''Are you okay with the idea? I mean, are you feeling all right? Was this what you wanted?''

"I don't know how I feel. I guess I just never gave it much thought. We certainly never did anything to prevent it!"

His smile was very knowing. "I'm well aware of that."

"You mean you did it on purpose?"

He shrugged, all innocence. "Who, me? Hey, I'm just a country boy. What do I know about— Ow!" he said, laughing, as she quickly moved around the table and punched him on the arm.

"You *wanted* me to get pregnant, you sneak!" she exclaimed, laughing as he pulled her down into his lap.

The kiss he gave her was filled with love and reassurance and a great deal of longing. When their lips finally parted, both of them were breathing erratically. "Here I've been...wondering how to...break the news, afraid you wouldn't...want a baby this soon," she admitted between breaths.

He sobered, his eyes filled with love as he studied her beloved face. "I can't think of anything that would please me more than for us to start our family now. I'll admit that I hoped you'd get pregnant sooner or later, but I figured that the law of nature would catch up with us eventually, so I wasn't giving it much thought." He hugged her to him. "And yes, this means that we are definitely going to get you a housekeeper. You're going to have to cut back on the heavy work, at least."

She cupped his face in her hands. "It's so hard for me to believe all of this. A year ago I thought we were going to lose the ranch. I didn't know what to do or where to go or what to plan. And then—" she kissed him "—you walked back into my life and nothing's been the same ever since."

He smoothed his hand across her flat abdomen. "Hey, babe, I have a hunch you haven't seen nothing yet!" His hand strayed to her breast and within a few minutes he'd picked her up and started for the stairs, her arms entwined around his neck.

Megan smiled to herself, thinking about the changes. As long as Travis was a part of her life, she knew she'd face all the changes with courage and calm acceptance. His love for her had finally helped her to understand what strength can be gained by accepting love and help from others.

* * * * *

Daughters of Texas continues next month with INSTANT MOMMY— *Mollie O'Brien's romance with her own lonesome cowboy. It is coming your way from Silhouette Romance—March's Bundle of Joy title. Don't miss it!*